*Penguin Books*
## *NIGHT ANIMALS*

*B*orn in Melbourne in 1947, Bruce Pascoe has lived most of his life in the
country. He is a teacher, education con-
sultant, writer and publisher. In 1982, he
established *Australian Short Stories*
quarterly magazine.

He has two children, to whom this book
is dedicated.

*Bruce Pascoe*

*NIGHT ANIMALS*

*Penguin Books*

Penguin Books Australia Ltd,
487 Maroondah Highway, PO Box 257
Ringwood, Victoria 3134, Australia
Penguin Books Ltd,
Harmondsworth, Middlesex, England
Penguin Books,
40 West 23rd Street, New York, NY 10010, USA
Penguin Books Canada Ltd,
2801 John Street, Markham, Ontario, Canada L3R 1B4
Penguin Books (NZ) Ltd,
182-190 Wairau Road, Auckland 10, New Zealand

First published by Penguin Books Australia, 1986
Reprinted 1986

Typeset in Garamond Book by Leader Composition Pty Ltd
Made and printed in Australia by The Book Printer, Maryborough, Victoria

Pascoe, Bruce, 1947-.
Night animals.
ISBN 0 14 008742 7.
I. Title.
A823'.3

For my children, Marnie and Jack

# *CONTENTS*

# *THYLACINE*

*I*n the Australian bush at night, you could find a lost sixpence or the feldspar in a piece of quartz, you could find the buckle off a dog's collar or a sooty owl in a tree. But you'd never find a pound note or an ant and you'd never find an old sepia photograph or why things are the way they are, although men will look for it there, and some of them all of their lives.

And so Douglas was looking again, even though he'd told his brother he was going to check the chooks. That cold winter luminescence shone with such a fierce white light. Ah, it's a cold star. A cold star bearing the steely light of a cold moon, bearing that light without blinking, allowing it to find old sixpences and feldspar, dog's buckles and sooty owls, but very little else. More than enough light for some things, but not enough for vision.

Old iron shines like new milled steel, a shovel blade glints sharp from the work in gravelly soil, trees shine like chandeliers, the dam like a disc of stamped plate. All these old things gleam anew. The barbed wire's rusty knots shine with frost, spider's webs are jewelled like the most precious things hung from the pale necks of the world's most desirable women.

Douglas checked the chooks and they stared at his eyes. Stupid chooks. He closed his fingers around the neck of a hen, and it blinked one eye but didn't move.

He checked the wire where he'd made the repair, and it was still intact. Six chooks they'd lost, and not a murmur. No feathers. No wild cackles. No fox dashing about in panic and blood lust. Just a chook off the roost and a neat hole in the wire. Douglas didn't know this animal. Clarrie said dingoes or native cats, but Douglas knew he didn't believe it himself. He knew the bush better than that, but Clarrie was the sort of bloke who always needed to propose a solution even if he knew it was wrong; anything to fill a gap.

When they'd found the human skulls, Clarrie had said it was just old timers caught in a fire, even though Clarrie must have seen the strangeness of the sockets. Old Pearson had died out in the bush, killed by a tree that slipped back off its stump and drove his leg into the ground. Pinned him there. The bull ants stripped him clean. Clarrie had seen Pearson's skull and must have seen the difference in these others, but he just rolled them away with his boot and said it must have been two old timers. Clarrie was like that.

Douglas saw the stones but didn't bother to tell Clarrie; he'd only argue back. So he'd returned later and picked them up and seen how the long one matched the hollow in the flat one. Douglas placed them in the crook of a tree near where the skulls had been found. Where he could put his hands on them again.

The brothers got on all right. They could put in a row of fence posts in a day and say no more than was needed to accomplish the task; and to put in a row of stringybark posts you don't need to say a lot. There's holes and posts and a straight line. If the posts ram tight, and the eye slips along the flat faces of each post, the job's done.

Douglas didn't need people. He sold the tickets at the local dance because it meant you could stand out on the verandah and listen to the blokes yarn and maybe add your piece about the last flood, but it was a way of meeting people without going through the bother of trying to balance a noisy china cup on a saucer and think of something to say at the same time.

And the women always made him nervous. And dancing. Dancing was plain impossible. He watched other blokes dance, blokes like him, bush workers, timber millers, cow cockies, and yet they could get around; some of them just glided about.

He'd watched the women's bodies like the other men, but he'd never really met one he wanted. During national service the boys had played up a bit, and that time he'd gone up to Candelo with the cricket team he didn't come back for three days. But not anyone you'd want to marry, stay with always; and anyway who'd have him? Short freckly bloke on a broken down dry ridge farm. Women round here knew where the gravel pits were.

He'd never asked Clarrie. He'd never asked Clarrie anything much. Clarrie wasn't the sort of bloke you asked anything of. He guessed that Clarrie had knocked about a bit. Those trips to Bombala to sell cows sometimes took a while, but Clarrie never seemed – never seemed lonely or anything. Clarrie always had everything worked out. Douglas thought he'd know if anything worried his brother. When the old man had died, Douglas had watched, stunned, as tears dropped out of his brother's eyes. Clarrie had wiped his face with a rag and said 'Dad taught me everything. All I know about the bush and that. That's all,' and again he had plunged his spade into the broken clay of the grave.

They got on all right, but there were times when Douglas liked to get away. The nights at the dances, the other blokes and the music, watching the women, and just something different. And nights like this, with the cold moonlight. He didn't tell Clarrie, you couldn't, but he knew some poems by heart. All the school books were still on the shelf.

Probably never occurred to Clarrie to throw them out. The sixth grade reader, *Modern Short Stories*, and that book of

French poems that came with their lounge suite at the clearing
sale.

He didn't feel like it tonight, but sometimes he'd said those
poems looking over the dam and down to the river: 'Slowly,
silently, now the moon/walks the night in her silver shoon . . .'
Shoon, shoon. He'd worked it out that it must be shoes. Their
teacher had just expected them to know, but then she was the
sort of jackass who'd never seen the paws of a sleeping dog in
the frosty moonlight. How many people had?

He'd worked out how to say some of the French poems, too.
He'd looked in amazement at the sheet music while cleaning
up after a dance one night and a folded sheet fell from the back
of a book, '*Non, je ne regrette rien.*' He wondered what it
meant, but he found '*Alouette, gentille Alouette*', and suddenly the words and the song snapped to the front of his brain
and he turned back to '*Non, je ne regrette rien*', and he
worked out how most of the words must sound; but he'd never
told Clarrie. Clarrie wasn't the sort of bloke you could.

What was that?

He didn't move. He didn't even let his heart beat any
differently after its initial hesitation. He could feel the hair on
his shoulders and across his neck edging upwards, but he
didn't move. There it was again. A growl like he'd never heard
before. He didn't allow his head to move, but his eyes
swivelled and saw it almost straight away. After all, he was a
bushman, and this was his yard, and his eyes found the strange
object in it instantly. And look at it! What an animal!

The beast had been looking at the house but felt the man's
eyes find his own, and they looked at each other, and the barbs
of glance hooked in eye flesh. Memories and visions are made
thus.

The animal was gone in the next instant, and Douglas knew
he'd be gone, but he followed him to the edge of the timber
and stopped by the fence. Douglas spoke and his voice, clear
and hard in the sharp white air, chased and found the beast.

'*Je vous regarde* – I saw you, dog, or – wolf. That's what you are. I saw you, tiger dog – Thylacine'. What a word to pitch into the moonlight.

Even as it ran, the animal heard the yelling and the strange word that was its name, and the sound would stay. Thylacine! It stood on the dry ridge among the shards of quartz and swung its heavy head to look down into the valley, knowing it was safe. Surely nothing could spirit itself through time so quickly. But a voice could, and did again.

'I know you're up there, tiger. I saw you.' The two knew each other. The wolf would remember the voice and the man would never forget the beast. In this universe of beings, these two were fused by the light of a silver moon. Both hearts beat; the tiger on the ridge, the man in the valley.

'I saw you, tiger.' There are some things, the man knew, which could never be denied. A man's spirit is built thus.

But animals are as logical as men, and Douglas had stood out in the bush where he knew the tiger must pass. The feldspar shone in the shafts of moonlight, the eucalypt leaves hung like small, bright scimitars of snipped tin, and the dog was there. Douglas could feel its presence by the way his hair crept beneath his collar.

'I know you're there, dog.' At the first word, before the muscles of the legs had flung the bones into flight, the animal's eyes had seen the other's eyes above where the voice had come out of the moonshine. 'I saw you, Thylacine. You can't deny that.'

Some night, man's logic and beast's logic diverged. The man knew he'd keep seeing it, although not so close to the house again. Chickens weren't that attractive. Not to a wild animal. Foxes and chickens were built for each other, but Tasmanian Tigers – well, they could take chickens or leave them, and when men were around, they left them.

But some nights, out of the bush came that quiet sound. No chase, no guns, just the sound. You looked out for things like that. You didn't get too close to snakes, you kept out of the way of eagles, and, especially, you kept out of the way of men.

But this one kept on being there. You never heard it; it was always where you couldn't smell it. And then, just that noise, not growling, just the same quiet sounds. No harm came, but you avoided things like that, if you could. It was better without the moon. The man wasn't there without the moon.

'Hey fellas, old Jack reckons he's seen a Tasmanian Tiger out by the river.' Bob Ridgeway had turned his big, red face over his shoulder to yell to the other blokes.

'Bull,' said Arnold Carter. 'Old Jack's been on the white lightning again.' Old Jack didn't like Carter, so he shut up.

'He just said so,' persisted Ridgeway. 'Didn't yer Jack; while you was settin' traps.' Jack didn't speak. His eyes were affirmative, but his shoulders looked as if his head was hoping its bloody mouth would stay shut.

'Keep the cork in the kero bottle, Jack,' said Carter, who knew how to use words like the whipping end of a roll of barbed wire. Jack flinched. 'Anyone else seen a Tasmanian Tiger?' Carter let the last words leer. No one spoke. Douglas shuffled the last few dance tickets, and the group began chuckling and slapping broad shoulders. Jack slipped out into the moonlight back to his camp. No one noticed. Silly old Jack, seein' bloody tigers now. Poor old coot. Trust bloody Arnold to stick in the boot, eh!

The last Palma Waltz bleated to a close, and the hall was packed up. Douglas cast an eye over the sheet music on the piano, but this new bloke didn't use the same stuff that the other pianist had used. Whatever happened to the other fella, Douglas wondered. Some blokes just disappear. Always a bit strange, that fella. Always quiet, never quite met your eyes. Except, every now and then while he was playing, he'd look up, and you'd catch him, and wonder what he was thinking. Not the Pride of Erin, that's for sure. Douglas wondered what *Non, je ne regrette rien* had meant. Could foreign words tell you anything more about a man?

With the new moon, the chooks began to disappear again.

Sometimes Douglas would wait for the tiger in the bush. He would crouch beside the river and wait for the dog to highstep through the shallows to hide its track. 'Hullo, Thylacine. I saw you again.' But you couldn't tramp around the bush every moonlit night pretending to track a chicken thief. Clarrie'd get sick of it.

In bed, Douglas would think of the tiger, those swift glances they had shared. They got to know each other. Douglas could see the dog's frustration in the glances now. 'Here's that man *again*.' It was almost like tipping your hat. The man would greet the beast with its name, and the beast would recognize the man, recognize the voice long before the end of the split second it took to find the eyes above the voice. The man became an annoyance, like a new-fallen log across an old path, an owl that snatches the bandicoot you've tracked all the way from the creek. To the tiger, the man became just another night animal, and the man knew it and revelled in that pride.

Douglas lay in bed with the moon on his face, the pillow like a field of snow. Yes, it was as though the beast no longer thought of him as a man, but as an animal of the night, a clever one that would sometimes appear. Not an enemy, but an equal, and strangely, Douglas's heart strained with a feeling like – then his throat went tight. He was proud, but it was more than that, it was almost like –.

The blast of the shotgun rattled the window pane by Douglas's face. He sat up in bed with that strange animal cry still with its hooks at his chest. He saw Clarrie with the shotgun. Clarrie turned and looked up at Douglas's moon-white face at the window.

'I just shot at a wild dog. It won't get far. There's enough blood over here to fill a bucket.' Clarrie came over to the window holding up a finger dipped in the blood.

'Thought I'd better do somethin' to stop you trampin' around the bush every night.' Douglas stared at the blood on Clarrie's finger and felt the hair prickling under his pyjama coat. The claw of the beast's cry slowly released, but now there was another sensation leaching from the wound the sound had made.

Moonlight nights were terrible after that. Douglas lay in bed, and the words of poems crept across his mind, trying to close up a wound with the soft stitches of the sounds and rhythms. If, in the eleven books the brothers owned, he'd found 'Tyger! Tyger! burning bright,' he would have read it to his heart and hoped that the words would heal.

But he didn't know those words and his mind sought for words that it didn't, couldn't know. If they'd had the seventh grade reader, he would have found it in there, but he didn't go to seventh grade. He was just a bushman.

# BLACK VELVET NIGHT

*B*ooraby walked along the beach striking his spear with the leaf of a cabbage palm. He wore large feathered shoes and his feet left no mark upon the sand. Looking straight ahead he struck the spear with the palm leaf and strode beside the waves.

Genoa Jack was yarding cattle while the boss leaned over the rails counting his brands. 'Okay, Jack, that'll do. Go and get the house cows.' 'Okay, boss.' Jack watched the boss walk off to the homestead and saw Birrawong coming with a billy of tea. As she passed the boss, Birrawong cast her eyes down and tried to cover her breasts with her arms. The white man muttered something as he went past, and when the girl looked up her eyes were dark with fear.

Jack watched the girl as he drank the tea and ate the hunk of cold damper. A baby cried and they both looked towards their shack. The girl silently went to the lean-to and brought out the child.

'Binda binda, Nargalilly,' crooned the mother. Jack finished the tea and looked back beyond the farm to the blue ranges which sloped down into the sea. Birrawong followed his gaze and said quietly, 'Murrang man comin', Jack.'

9

Booraby walked along the beach with his feet and eyes straight ahead, and now he was chanting the totem. 'Murra Murra Murra, Labilla Labilla, Murra Murra Murra, Labilla, Labilla.'

The eyes of dingoes in the dunes, emus in the shadows of the forest edges and the sea eagle in the cloud towers of the sky saw the man, heard his song, and watched him out of sight.

Jack rode off to bring up the cows, glancing up at the ranges. On his way back, he saw a koala with a young one clinging to its back in the crook of a gum, 'Kayala Kayala . . .' Jack involuntarily began to chant. He was shaken by the sight of his woman's totem so far from its usual home. 'Kayala Kayala Boondella Dirill Dirilla,' his mind sang, and he spurred his horse to rid himself of the old thoughts. As he neared camp, he began to sing a white man's song. 'Send her victarious, habby and glarious, long ray-a-ane overus, God save em Gween.' 'Shut up Jack, ya black bastard,' a stockman shouted from the yard. Jack laughed until he saw Birrawong standing beside the hut with the piccaninny. She didn't speak, but through her eyes he could see her mind chanting, 'Murra man comin', Murra man comin'.' His laugh faded, and he walked across and struck her face. 'Bugger them bloody totems. All bullshit, I told ya. Bugger that Murrang man. He's not gonna walk up here and take ya back. Let 'em chant by them bloody fires. I'm not scared 'a black songs. Them all shit, see.'

He unbuckled the girths and, as he bent behind the horse out of sight of his wife, he sang the anthem in a loud and careless voice, but his eyes were on the blue ranges. 'God save 'em grayous Gween, God save 'em grayous Gween . . .'

'Shut that shit, Jack,' shouted a voice from the stables. 'Black man singing white songs, our song.'

'Murra Murra Murra, Labilla Labilla,' chanted Booraby as he moved through the tea-tree groves at the edge of the beach. His hand rested on the top rail of the fence. He saw the cows

and the kangaroos in the paddock as he stalked the edge of the
clearing behind the homestead.

'Get that Birrawong gin in here to iron these clothes, Arthur.
I'll have to look after baby.' The white woman mopped up the
baby's vomit as she spoke. 'And tell her to sleep by the stove in
here tonight. And tell her to wear a clean frock.'

Birrawong came when she was called and tried to cover
herself from the boss's gaze as she walked past him into the
house. Genoa Jack rolled himself in his blanket, but his eyes
stared into the darkness.

Booraby's lips moved silently, and he struck the spear with
the palm leaf and rubbed it across his brow and over his groin
and at last plaited the palm to the end of the shaft.

'Aya aya aya Murrang gidoon. Aya aya aya.' The white people
heard the high-pitched moaning and came to the opening of
the hut, some with soap on their faces, others rubbing sleep
from their eyes. Jack lay staring at the roof of the humpy, the
spear through his breast pinning him to the soil. The
crumpled palm leaf barely stirred at the end of the shaft.

All that day the men stood in groups around the yards
talking of the blacks. They had all heard stories of black men
who started killing. The women stood on the verandah
watching the men and listening to the gin. The piccaninny
Nargalilly howled, as a child howls, unconscious of events but
aware of the fates.

The white men knew that Genoa Jack had been killed
because he had taken a woman. They knew that the black
would return for the girl and would probably still be watching
the camp.

At last the white boss came over. He eyed her breasts as he
stepped inside the humpy. 'We've decided to look after the
piccaninny here until this black man is found.' The boss bent
and picked up the child. He knelt on one knee and palmed the
girl's breasts and ground at her lips with his mouth. He struck

her, and she sank to the floor, her swollen lips trembling over the words of her totem song. 'Murrang Murrang, Bindalla Bindalla.'

The piccaninny was to be kept in the back room of the homestead and the lubra out in the bush. The kookaburras' last song stilled the evening and everyone at the farm waited for the dark – and the black man – to come.

In the bush, Booraby crouched on his heels watching. He took a stone from a bag tied to his waist and licked paste from it.

As dusk began to draw out the shadows, Birrawong suckled her child. When they took the child from her, she walked past the men to the edge of the forest. She made her fire in a small clearing out of sight of the farm and sat cross legged by the fire. On the verandah the men saw the smoke rise in white moonlight.

Booraby watched the girl by the fire as she swayed and keened her totem. As Booraby's words began her song shuddered. 'Aya aya, Murrang gidoon,' Booraby's foot beat in the sand. The moon silvered the leaves and cast a cold white lace upon the fern of the forest floor. His hands moved in a patch of light like moths caught in a jar, fluttering, as he murmured his song. An owl called in the bush. 'Boo book, boo book.' So slow.

At last he walked into the clearing and took off his hair belt, drew it across her back and pressed her gently to the ground.

The shot cracked open the starlight. The Boobook stopped. White men stepped into the clearing. The girl looked at them and then turned away. Blood brimmed from their chests. 'Jesus, you've hit the girl,' one voice said.

Beside the clearing the Boobook began to call again. 'Boo book, boo book, boo book.' So tired. In the white of the night, a child cried. So alone.

# *FLOUR FOR YOUR GRAVE*

*I*t was a small white cottage with a front verandah and windows looking over the lake and ocean. The moon spread a train of white gauze across the sea, across the lake and partly lit the gaunt face of the man who stood with his hand on the verandah rail.

His head was huge, leonine, faded tawny hair. The skull showed through the skin so that, half lit by the paleness of moonlight, it had the bleaching of bones you find in sand.

Inside the house, a woman sat by the fireplace with a Bible on her lap. Her face was lit so that her dull hair and cheeks were gilded. A lamp on the table cast light on the Bible. Each time she turned a page she would glance to a corner of the room where a baby slept and then at the closed door.

McKenzie was looking at the fire which burnt at the shore of the lake. In the glimmer the figures stamped the earth and sang the corroboree, and the call of night birds was intoxicated by the perfume of pittosporums.

McKenzie went inside and the door slammed behind him. He took a newspaper off the mantelpiece and spread it in the lamplight. His wife looked up. He had read this page to her several times.

13

His hands bunched until he was resting his weight on his knuckles. He flung the paper from the table and a page settled by the cot. The woman said nothing.

'There's going to be trouble. This is exactly what happened before. Singing and dancing and then the murder of those Glenaladale people.'

He sat down opposite his wife and began to roll a cigarette. This man was her husband, the father of her children; the one who provided.

That morning, she had lugged her clothes from the copper with a length of tea tree and wrung them with hands the colour of boiled crabs. Each time she reached to the line, she saw the Aborigines on the edge of the lake.

From her house the bush grass sloped down to a flat beside a scallop of the lake. She thought of it as the perfect picnic spot. An English lake; green grass, wildflowers, drooping trees, children laughing.

Between the damp washing she watched the old women playing with the babies. Earlier she had seen the men leave. They had been laughing quietly and jostling each other. Their smiles for each other were wide, but when they looked at her there was nothing.

The lubras were up to their waists in the water, feeling with their toes for the blood mussels and oysters. She couldn't help looking at their bodies glistening with water as they splashed each other. The breasts of the young girls joggled, pearled with water and sunlight.

As she watched them she remembered a painting in the Sydney gallery. Naked women by a lake. Now, watching the bodies, she remembered that lushness.


McKenzie tossed the butt into the fire. 'Something will have to be done. Weatherby's stockman says some kind of witch doctor is coming down from up north.'

She watched him.

14

'Sounds like they're getting up a war party, to me. Pearson reckons a couple of his sheep have disappeared. That's the way it usually starts: a few sheep, a dog, then a whole family.'

His huge hands clapped on his knees. 'Well it's not going to happen here. It's too dangerous.'

McKenzie lay awake listening to the click of the sticks, the bull roarer, the chant. His wife beside him slept and dreamt of a picnic where a mother handed out raisin cakes beside a perfect lake.

Eric Cousins had a forge behind his shack. Most of the men had gathered there this morning with broken shovels, plough shares, a pouch of tobacco, or just a nervous disinclination to work.

While Cousins beat the glowing steel and his son strained at the bellows, the men talked of the corn crop, kangaroos on the winter pastures, the price of pumpkin seeds and at last, the Aborigines. Some of the farmers were edgy and scared; a couple had avaricious eyes on the pastures around the lake. They leant against the fence, their eyes in the shadow of their hats and their faces in tobacco smoke.

Harold Durkin, the fisherman whose family first settled the lake, said that it was nonsense. The time for initiation of the young bucks, nothing more.

'Happens every five years, or so, and there's half a dozen uninitiated young blokes in the camp. Dad gave 'em a bag of flour for the last corroboree. Isn't that right, Dad?'

Old Clive's mottled hands stripped bark from a twig. Clive was nearly blind and rarely spoke. His eyes were clear, washed pale by the sea and, when he looked up, the others waited.

'Yeah, that's right,' and he continued to expose the clean, green wood between the callouses of his fingers.

'See, I told yah,' his son persisted, 'this black fella is just comin' down for the initiation. He always comes down. What's his name, Dad?' Clive didn't look up.

15

'Nullica.'

Tom Mullins leant forward and spoke, 'That's right, what old Clive says. Nullica comes through every once in a while to initiate all the boys. And besides we've never had any trouble with our blacks.'

'That's all very well,' broke in McKenzie, as he pulled the newspaper cutting from his pocket and waved it towards Tom Mullins, 'but this tells how those blacks chopped up the Connollys at Glenaladale. A few sheep and dogs and then a whole family; I reckon something's up.'

'Who's lost sheep?' Tom Mullins demanded.

'Pearson has,' McKenzie said, and they all looked at Pearson, a small man whose eyes never quite met the eyes of anyone else.

Pearson coughed.

'I've lost four now, and those blacks have been walking through my property every morning.' Tom Mullins looked at him carefully and spoke quietly, trying to fix the other man's shifting glance.

'You're sure it's not dogs?' Tom continued to watch Pearson, whom he had never liked. Pearson was cruel to the blacks in small ways, had tried to buy young lubras and everyone knew that he wanted the piece of land that bordered the lake.

Furtively, Pearson pulled something out of his pocket and held it up.

'I found this and a few others in the paddock.' They all looked at the sheep's foot. An excited murmur passed among the men and McKenzie spoke again.

'I reckon we've got to drive 'em out; they're up to no good. We've got women and kids to think of as well as our animals. The sheep don't matter so much, but what about your kids, eh?' He searched each face in turn and, as each man's gaze was met, they shifted their feet, all except Mullins who stared straight back and old Clive Durkin who didn't even look up.

'I reckon we should give 'em another bag of flour,' said

Pearson, and his eyes had a hard, horrible glint. The look of a treacherous dog, thought Mullins. The other man knew of stories where black men had been presented with gifts of spiked flour; some of the men were ashamed, some were uneasy and a few thought of extended pasturage. Old Clive Durkin looked towards Pearson, straightened stiffly, and walked from the group. Tom Mullins spat at Pearson's feet and followed.

The two spoke quietly with their heads down as the rest of the group of men watched them. McKenzie, not willing to lose control, began to speak again and they crowded around to read his scrap of newspaper.

Mrs McKenzie watched the men bringing back the possums and wallabies they had killed. The youngest boy carried six black ducks, three in each hand, and every few steps he had to trot to keep up with the long stride of the older men.

The woman suckled her child. As the baby's face relaxed, she heard the sound of voices and the scrape of the store shed door. She could hear her husband, Pearson's unmistakably reedy voice, and a couple of others.

Tom Mullins and Clive Durkin saddled up two of Tom's horses and took the bush track along the river. They said little to each other but called in at some farms along the way and spoke first to the black stockmen and then to the white farmers.

In the purple of dusk they watered the horses at the edge of the river, and Tom took his hat off and wiped the sweat from his brow with the sleeve of his shirt. Old Clive was tired and slumped against a tree, his restless fingers crumbling dry leaves and bark. One of the horses stamped softly, and Tom looked up to see the black man wading across the river, his spears and tucker bag above his head.

The men greeted each other formally. Nullica and Clive

spoke to each other in Kurnai, and then Tom explained the restlessness among the white men. They remounted with Nullica on the back of Clive's horse and all the way back Tom heard the murmuring rise and fall of their voices. He'd never heard the old fisherman say so much.

The moon was on the lake and ocean and the fire burned brightly, but the singing and dancing of the feast night had stopped. The uninitiated boys who had not been allowed to join in the feast ran from one stricken man to the next. They wailed and moaned among the stiffening corpses of their brothers and sisters, the old men and the mothers, the tribesmen and the babies.

The boys tugged at their hair and moaned, breaking occasionally into the songs of lament. They were too afraid to leave the camp for fear of the dark and the evil spirit that had brought this sickness. All night they huddled around the fire, and gradually they calmed and examined the flour bag and a resolution steadied their hearts and turned grief into a harder thing.

All night McKenzie listened to the wails and screams and all night his hand held the barrel of his gun as he sat by the fireplace, his ears trembling with the concentration of his listening. His wife stared at the ceiling as she lay rigid in the bed, listening to the terrible cries in the night. She remembered the laughing of the women in the water and the young men with the wallabies and ducks; she remembered the scraping of the store shed door and began shivering, until at last she took the Bible in her hands and without opening that book her lips whispered, 'How long shall the land mourn, and the herbs of the field wither, for the wickedness of them that dwell therein . . .' She stopped, conscious of her husband in the doorway and once again the moonlight sought his face and revealed the hard bone beneath the skin.

\* \* \*

The men gathered around the forge as the last of the sunrise paled in the sky above the blue ranges. They watched the three horsemen ride past them to the edge of the lake.

Nullica slid from the horse's back and walked into the camp. The young men were gone. Nullica didn't bend down to the bodies, but his lips moved and Clive turned away, his leather face beaded with tears.

Tom Mullins marched up to McKenzie's house. He entered the kitchen and called McKenzie's name. Mrs McKenzie's eyes stared at him as if surprised that the spear pinning her to the door should be in her chest, or perhaps it was the look of a mother who had seen the head hewn from her baby.

Tom noticed the black book opened on the table and while his stomach retched and his eyes wept, his soul was like iron. He tossed the book into the embers of the fire and even as the flames gathered and licked at the pages which spoke of the sin and righteousness in men, he could hear the weary lament of the black man. A sound like the sigh of wind in trees, that ancient wind that has always wreathed this globe, carrying in its path the stench of death from a thousand centuries, the wind that even now stirred the hair of the black man by the lake edge, the fisherman by his side and the men at the forge, the same wind that gathered the smoke from the cottage chimney into the vastness of the world. The wind that becomes the gale that beats and batters at the homes of men and shrieks and wails in their ears. The wind is old, older than the black man, or the white man. The wind forgets nothing and seeks to remind us all.

# COBBER:
## Peach Face

*E*very Thursday morning he heard the clink of bottles out in the street. The old ladies. Cobber dragged the covers away and pushed his legs into pants. He was just in time to grab four bottles from the kitchen as the old ladies wheeled their pram to his terrace gate.

They would mutter thanks in their threadbare voices. They always did. But this morning the smaller sister was fumbling with a pack of Marlboro, pushing a cigarette in her mouth, slightly askew. She was excited and clumsy with the sudden gift left on a dustbin lid. Like a kid with an unexpected bun from the baker.

And then there were no matches. Her hands fluttered at the sides of her dress and her eyes dashed in panic at the taller sister. No matches.

'Have ya got a light, sir?' said the taller.

His heart shrank from the title. He fled indoors and brought back a lighter and held it to the trembling cigarette. The taller sister thanked him; the shorter gulped in the smoke, too intent now to acknowledge anything. He watched them walk up the street sharing their windfall fag. Savouring the blue air down to the filter. He watched as they butted the cigarette and reassembled their act. The taller pushed the pram, and the smaller stacked the bottles where she was told. The smaller sister was too rattled to think. She stumbled from succour to succour under the steadier hand of her sister. His eyes followed their ragged caravan until it disappeared around the hotel corner. What happens when one of them dies? Maybe this is just one more routine hastily worked up by two old hoofers after one or both have lost their straight man. A small death.

At work Cobber surveyed the piles of rubbish that had come down from the chutes. He turned over the broken china and solitary shoes. Twenty-six and picking over what others had thrown away. He worked alone in the rubbish room of a shopping complex. Uncertain messages from the other world. One sandshoe. Loaves of bread. A perfect dress. Tins of paint. He would stand before the despatches and try to unravel the code. Faulty, bad, broken, unsaleable? Cobber clothed himself from the spleen, the mistakes and the imperfections of the others. He knew one of them. A young bloke who worked in the licensed grocer and sometimes sent down tins of food or a bottle of sherry and, most Christmases, a bottle of Scotch.

He turned the dials of the furnace, cleared the flue, and began shovelling the rest of the piles. As he came across vegetables and bread, he kicked them towards the door.

The chook man brought his cart every day to fill it with waste food. The door of the furnace room would scrape open, and Harry would wheel in his cart. A box on a pram frame. They'd nod, and Harry would clear his throat and pile the stuff into his cart and go. On his first visit, he pointed at the bread. 'For me chooks,' he said. Cobber nodded, and that was that.

The shovel scooped into the piles of paper, plastic and cardboard and the furnace engulfed them in flames. The chook man came, scraped the door, nodded, loaded his goods and left, the signal that it was nine o'clock and morning tea time. Cobber picked up a toy from the rubbish. One that you wind up by pushing down the driver's head. Cobber pushed it. No go. Spring's broke.

A flurry of boxes dropped into a pile of rubbish and something flew out. Really flew. The coffee was half way to his lips when he saw the whirr of wings.

Cobber put down his coffee and walked to the pile where the bird had disappeared. Grey, orange face. A budgerigar. No, too big. Parrot? They eyed each other. Cobber stalked the bird. It fluttered clumsily among the boxes, and Cobber, with equal clumsiness and determination, hunted it.

At last the bird was engulfed in the hand and a finger stroked chest and head. How do you comfort a trapped bird?

Cobber put the bird in the dark of his bag and went upstairs to the pet shop. There he saw the companion bird. Same eyes. Same terror.

'What do you call those parrots?' he asked.

'Peach Face,' said the woman looking at his overalls.

'What do they eat?'

'Seeds and fruit.'

'Ah,' said Cobber, aware of her distaste: 'I've seen your rubbish lady. Give us a packet of seed and a cage then.'

'Do you have a bird, sir?' Was her eye putting two and two together?

'Nah, but me Mum has. Thought I'd buy her a new cage and some tucker for her birthday.' Anyone with a brain or a laugh in their bones would want to know who was having the birthday. But the shop assistant didn't; just gave back the change and held out the cage and seed. Money in till. Hands washed.

Cobber's mother was blind, and she stood in front of the cage. 'It's a Peach-Faced Parrot, Mum. Flew down the chute at work yesterday. It's grey with an orangey yellow face. Doesn't say boo.' Not much good to a blind woman, thought Cobber, and led his mother into the Saturday morning sun of the street. A walk in the park, he thought, trying to entertain the mother he rarely saw.

'How are ya, chief?' The man who spoke was just entering his gate. Cobber's neighbour.

'Not bad, Terry. How are you?'

'Not bad.' Mother and son walked on.

'That's me neighbour, Mum. Ex-boxer, nose all over his face. Had the shit belted out of him. Walks with a stumble. Holds his arms funny. Seems to be on a forward lean all the time.' Cobber's words fell into the rhythm of their blind and ushering feet. 'Collects paper and stuff. You always see him in the streets with some parcel or other, scuttling off home. His room's full of it. And cats. He's got about eight cats and sits there among his piles of paper and bits and pieces watching a little black and white telly. Three cats in his lap, one on the window sill, one on the TV, everywhere. You can see him through the window. Every day.'

'Always says the same thing. "How are ya, chief." And he's always not bad. Well, neither am I, I'm not bad either.' Cobber looks at his Mum. Her blind eyes look as if they struggle to believe him.

As they pass a hotel, he points to a little dog chained to the fire hydrant. 'That's Alec's dog, Mum. Mate of mine. He's a cleaner at the Salvo hall.' The door swings open and there's Alec, wire haired, short blue tongue like a cockatoo's.

'Hullo Alec. How are ya?'

'Not bad, Cobber, just had a little pick me up before the wife puts me down.' His eyes looked as if his mind had tried to rev up a chuckle but the heart wasn't in it and the hard blue tongue swept the lips.

'Alec, this is me Mum.'

'Hullo Mrs Carter, how are you?'

'Good thanks.'

Alec untied the dog capering at his feet. The dog thought Alec was the best man in the world. Worth waiting for.

They walked around the strip of grass that represented the local park, and Cobber told his mother about the trees, the kids on bikes, the dogs rolling on their backs and biting at capeweed flowers.

She ate what her son cooked up, and went home. She didn't

ask him why he didn't come and live with her; she hadn't asked that for years. She could get by. She knew her way around her kitchen and the shops. She was all right, but she wondered about him.

'Since when have you liked budgies?' asked his mate as they sat among their beer bottles and dishes.

'It's a Peach Face.'

'Well, a bloody Peach Face, then. Since when have you been an animal lover?'

'You never knock back gifts from heaven, mate. That's what I say.'

'Well, who's going to look after it, then?'

'Listen, Ted, I'll look after the bloody bird, you just have another beer. That's what you're good at.'

'Christ, mate, we have enough trouble looking after ourselves in this dump without worrying about a bloody bird.' Ted poured another two glasses of beer and grumbled, 'What do we call it, seeing as we look like sharing a house with it?' Cobber took his beer and sucked away the froth.

'Telex.'

'What?'

'Telex. That's what we'll call it. Might talk, yer never know.'

'God love a duck, Cobber, what's got into you? Nothing wrong with Polly is there? Telex. You're a couple of shingles short, mate.'


But it didn't talk. Cobber and the bird stared at each other. It never ate, or never when you watched it. And never said anything. Not a sound. Just stared. After flying from one world to another, it had found them much the same, nothing remarkable, nothing worthy of song.

Cobber read a book on exotic birds. He pressed a finger against a page and looked up at the bird.

'It says here that you're from the jungle. What's the jungle like, eh? Dark? Wet? Big? Things bite ya?' The bird didn't respond. It would only scratch its ear when you turned away. You could hear the sound and catch the flurry from the corner of your eye, but when you turned it was sitting still on the perch. Staring.

'Well, are they better than this then? Plenty to eat. Friends. No bars. Warm, safe.' Cobber stood up to come at eye level. 'Tell me, is it better?'

He plumped down into the chair and flipped through the book and scanned the chapter on aviculture. He clapped it shut and threw it on the table. The bird had probably been born in a cage. Never knew a jungle. Wouldn't know one if it flew over it.

Ted came in flushed from a day at the races. 'Hyperno, mate. Hyperno. It's a bloody bird, I tell you. Bloody beautiful beast. Look, mate. Won enough to pay the rent for a month and do a round of the pubs.'

They did. Played pool, drank beer, laughed, watched the barmaid. Tingled as she turned and cocked her head seeing them watching her. Dared them. They didn't. She was beautiful. Untouchable. They weren't. Small men, blunt faces, coarse clothes, no quick phrases.

They left at closing with an armful of cans and sat on a park bench. They sang the Muddy Waters songs they both knew. Dylan. Josh White, Earl Hines.

> Prayers I send to heaven above
> 'Bout this burden I must bear.
> Nothin' much appeals to me
> Travellin', travellin'
> All alone.

'Shit mate, what has Kamahl got that we haven't?' asked Ted.

Cobber was staring into the treetops, his head resting on the back of the bench.

'What's a jungle?' he asked.

'Eh?'

'What's a jungle?'

'A lot of trees, mate.' Ted considered his response more thoroughly. 'A lot of big, wet trees.'

Cobber stood up. 'Well, I'm going to one.'

'It's a bit of a way, Cobber. You might have to cut a sandwich or two if you're gunna walk.' Ted looked up at his mate.

'Well, listen. I'm giving rubbish the flick for a week. You look after me bird while I'm gone and when I come back I'll tell ya what a jungle is.'

'That's bloody good of ya Cob. It's been on me mind for a while. Jungles and that. I wake up in the night thinking of the Amazon. A beautiful one too.' Ted giggled to himself and rolled a joint. As he licked the paper, he could see Cobber's back walking home through the park. He shrugged and lit up. Blowing out the smoke he felt his back ease into the bench slats. 'Jungle,' he laughed. 'Poor old Cobber, silly as a bloody wheel.'

The truck driver shared Cobber's cans and grass. 'Jungle, ya say. Ya wanna go to a jungle. Not Cairns or Townsville, a jungle.' He sighed. 'Well, yer easy pleased, mate; not like most people. I've always wanted to go to the Bahamas. Smoke cigars by the pool. Have black women demand a fuck.' His voice was dreamy, tasting the other world. 'Well I could do without the Bahamas I suppose, and the cigar . . . and I can't swim anyway.' He smiled at Cobber. Cobber stared out the window.


Ted was basically right thought Cobber as he walked back along the forest path. Lots of big, wet trees. A jungle is ferns, vines, secretive birds, sleepy pythons, and lots of big, wet mossy trees.

There was no suggestion of letting the bird go in this one, anyway. And they couldn't talk about it together. Telepathize about lush greenness. Telex had no ticker tape.

On the way back he got as far as the Genoa Hotel on the border and was ten cents short for a beer.

'Double or nothing,' he said to the barman. 'I'll flip ya for a beer.' Cobber went to toss a coin.

'Hang on,' said the barman, 'use this one, fairer that way.' Cobber tossed it, and the barman called tails.

'Heads, old son. Looks like I owe you two pots. May as well keep the coin too. Could bring ya luck.' Cobber had already noticed its two heads.

'Thanks, mate,' said Cobber. A dying breed he thought to himself as he walked to the phone and put in his three good coins.

'Ted, that you, Ted? Listen, mate, I'm stuck in a little bush town with no money. What about sending a few quid to the post office here. Good on ya, mate. Eh? What's that? Oh, nah, nah, can't be helped mate. Yeah, see ya.'

'Bad news?' asked the barman as Cobber returned to the bar for his second pot.

'Not really, I suppose. Me bird got out of its cage. Me mate tried to catch it, but it flew up into a big tree. A magpie got it.'

'Bit of bad luck. What kind was it?'

'Peach Face.'

'Ah, knew a bloke who had a couple. Sort of parrot aren't they.'

'Yeah. This one didn't talk, didn't fly, didn't do much at all.'

'Know the kind. Seen a lot like that in here. Bar parrots. Most of 'em can talk, but. Pity. Nothin' to say.' He winked at Cobber and placed a third pot in front of him.

'This one's for the Peach Face.'

Cobber saluted the barman with his full glass and as he sipped from it he saw the rubbish room in the bubbles. The waste repository of the other world. He downed the glass and decided not to go back. To settle for something that wasn't under or other. Neither jungle nor cage.

# COBBER
## The Cat Men of Genoa

*S*o Cobber stayed in Genoa.

On the strength of the few quid his mate had sent him he hired a van in the caravan park. All laminex, vinyl and crook fridge.

The barman gave him a job in the pub kitchen after asking him what he could cook. 'Chops and veg? Spot on, mate. That's all we eat here. Here's an apron. Eight bucks an hour, free tucker and a few sly pots. Done?'

'Done,' said Cobber. So here he was. No more underground work in the city. Out of the guts and into the kitchen. Ah well, least it's quiet.

After work he walked down to the beach and looked at the ocean, which he hadn't seen since he was a kid. Bit like a jungle, really. Wet. But nothing like the jungle he'd come from.

He worked alone in the kitchen. Never saw the bloke he replaced. 'Just went,' said the barman, 'just up and went. He went, and you came. Simple. One and one, and you've still got one. Life's maths.' The barman was a thinker. Have to watch him, thought Cobber scraping congealed fat into a bin.

28

'The fat of the land,' said Cobber to the cat. 'Hop into it, and good luck to you.'

The bloke who ran the service station across the road was an Italian who wore thongs and had a huge thirst.

'Hey, mister,' said the Italian as Cobber placed the counter tea in front of him. 'What's this shit you serve up?'

'Chops and veg,' replied Cobber.

'Ah, you're right, mister, there's the chop. That must be the veg.'

'Yeah, I always put the chop on the left-hand side. Saves confusion.'

Cobber put down the knives and forks wrapped in a paper napkin and walked towards the kitchen.

'New bloke,' said the barman. 'Started yesterday.'

'It's hard to tell, mister. He cooks just like the other bloke.' The Italian roared with laughter.

'Tell you what, mister,' the Italian said a few days later, 'you can have one of the vans at the back of my place for ten bucks a week as long as you help on the pumps when I go to town.' He pronounced town with capital letters. 'That's all, okay, but don't cook. You eat your chops and veg, and I'll eat mine. Okay?'

Seemed fine to Cobber, so he moved his sports bag over to the caravan. It had no glass in the windows, just like the van next to it. A man came out and smiled. Short, sandy hair.

'G'day,' said Cobber. The man put four fingers across his mouth, lifted his eyebrows and made a noise in his throat.

The next night, as Cobber drank in the bar after serving the teas and cleaning the kitchen, Carlo the Italian pulled up a stool.

'Hiya, mister. Looks like I can't avoid your chops and veg. I must be addicted,' he said holding his throat for effect. The barman stumped two pots in front of them and winked. 'Sly ones,' he whispered.

'Scotty,' Carlo said, 'that's the bloke in the van next to yours. He's dumb. No speak. Good bloke though, cuts timber in the bush, likes to have a yarn, wave his arms and make a noise. Talk about the weather to him. He's good at that. Picks the flood for us three weeks in advance. And don't knock his cats around. He'll take to you with his axe.'

They both had cats. Everywhere. Some shared Cobber's van. He brought back the kitchen waste and doled it out to the whole mob. Scotty watched him with tears in his eyes and tapped him on the breastbone with a wood-blackened finger making the sign of the cross on Cobber's heart. He clasped Cobber's hands and pointed to the sky and made a heh heh heh laughing sound, eyes sparkling.

'Rain?' inquired Cobber thinking of the floods. Scotty nearly shook his head off.

'Sun?' said Cobber thinking he had to get it this time. He did. Scotty nearly danced he was that pleased. Jigged and waved his arms and went, 'Heh heh heh.' So pleased to talk. So pleased to live near someone who liked cats. Scotty pointed to the cats and made the sign of the cross over Cobber again. Cobber hated cats. Always had. But for the blessing of a dumb man he could make an effort.

One Monday night, when the wind hurled hard pellets of rain at the windows, Carlo and Cobber sat by the fire playing cards with the barman.

The door opened and a man in elastic-sided boots and dry-as-a-bone weather cape came into the bar.

'Good night for it,' said the barman getting up. 'Have a beer, Kev?'

'Too right, I will,' said Kevin.

'What have you been up to, then?' the barman asked, putting the beer on the sopping towel.

'Oh, been up the farm counting me cows.' Carlo and the barman laughed. 'Kevin here's got a bit of bush that he's trying

30

to turn into a farm. Has trouble with his stock. Has to count it each night.'

'Any more livestock and I'll need a computer,' Kevin said after he'd drained a glass.

'This is a new bloke in town,' said Carlo.

'Good luck to ya, mate. You could do worse than this. What ya doin' for a crust or is the government doin' that for ya?' Cobber's clothes always gave him away.

'I'm cooking in the kitchen here.'

'Jesus, six counter teas a night'll make ya fortune. Be able to set up a boutique for gentlemen's fashions.' All but Cobber laughed.

'Just a joke mate,' said Kevin. 'You look no different than any other bloke on the road to me. Ever filleted a flathead?' Cobber looked at him. 'Flathead, mate. I work down at the fish factory when I'm not engaged in agricultural computation. Feel like filletin' fish? The other bloke I worked with took off to grow marijuana in the hills. More money in it. No bones. What do ya say? Still have time to rustle up tucker for Bill here.' Seemed fine to Cobber.

Getting the meat off flathead turned your hands into bloated red cushions, but while the weather was good the money was tolerable and the men and women at least knew how to laugh. Even if it was usually at the expense of someone with a wet flathead down the back of their shirt.

And besides that there was Mary. He'd never spoken to her. They nodded each day as they took up their positions on the conveyor belt. She scaled, he filleted. He paired with Kevin, the gun, so Cobber had to go flat out, but it still didn't stop him watching Mary as she swept the scaling knife back and forth. Fillets flopped into bins and skeletons sloshed into gut buckets, but his eye never missed a movement as she pushed her hair into place with the back of her forearm or removed a rubber glove to pick a scale from her lip.

After three days Kevin tallied up their work and collected their pay from the boss. Equal shares. 'Not bad cleaning for a

cook,' said Kevin as he passed over the notes. 'If you buy me a
beer, I might let you drench the cow at the weekend.' Cobber
did. He drenched the cow, fished for bream in the rivers with
Bill and Kevin, shot rabbits with Scotty (one for you, one for
me, one for the cats, all in signs) and was invited to the golf
club dance.

There was Mary. No rubber gloves, no fish. Same black hair.
Same eyes. Lashes. Lips. He swallowed beer at the bar and
watched as Carlo swept her around the dance floor. He could
dance, the big Italian. Light on those huge feet, but he spoilt
the grace by hooting with laughter and singing the words to all
the music. In Italian.

'Hey, mister,' he yelled, spinning towards him, 'you dance
with this girl, I'll get us all big drinks.' He left them there calling across the heads. 'Hey there, mister, three big cold drinks
and hurry, I can smell the police.'

Scotty could smell the rain, Carlo could smell the law.
Cobber could smell her hair as they danced. Bush dancing.
You hold each other and show the graces that farming and
fishing never allow. Huge hands with only the back of the
thumb pressed gently against women whose work might be
milking cows, chipping potatoes or scaling fish.

His nose was close enough so that when they waltzed her
hair brushed his nostrils. His head swam. Carlo held aloft
three giant drinks. All different colours. Silly drinks. Drinks
for a party. They sat at a table, Cobber and Mary stealing
glances at each other. Carlo looked at them.

'Holy Mother, I go to get drinks and I come back and no one
talks to me. Hey Kevin,' Carlo yelled, 'Do I stink? These two
won't talk to me anymore?'

'You don't stink mate, you're too loud to stink.' Kevin
laughed and nudged his mates who turned to look as Cobber
and Mary began dancing again.

Women in the hall put down their glasses to stare. Groups of
men turned, watching the waltz. Smiles, whispered com-
ments, excitement. Love. There was love in the air. It

gladdened the room even if it broke a few men's hearts. Even the most calloused hearts were charmed. A charm that for some would cause the hard pain of loss, of waste, for others it might quicken for a while the shared flesh, make the animal hairs stiffen on the backs of necks. That was the dance; the celebration.

They all danced. Wheeled about the floor. Made the musicians rest their arms in between numbers, knowing that they wouldn't get out the door before two. Even the copper knew if he turned off the grog tonight he'd be found in someone's fishing net tomorrow.

They laughed outside in the stars. Arms found waists or more bottles. Cobber didn't notice the nudges as they walked from the hall together.

They stood on a headland above the estuary and, yes, there was a moon and it did spread shimmering foil across the water and turned the boiling crests of waves into its own luminescence.

After washing up the last of the dishes from lunch next day, Cobber leant on the bar as Bill passed across a sly one.

'Bill,' he said, 'can I have a couple of days off?'

'Sure thing, mate. Where are you off to? Not going for too long I hope.'

'I'm going fishing up the river.'

'On yer own mate, just you and the fish?'

'Ar no. I'm going with Mary from the factory.'

Bill hesitated as he pushed a tray of glasses into the washer. 'Ah, well, in that case, hang on a tick.' He left the room and came back with a large bottle. 'You'll need one of these then, me boy. She likes this. French champagne, mate. Moët, nothing better.'

Cobber watched Bill's face, holding himself still. Feeling the electricity. 'She was my wife, Cobber. It's okay, mate. We've been separated for five years. She just cooked here to help me out. We're mates, friends, you know those things that – here take it, I'm not crook on you, I'm just – well, forget it, piss off, take yer French booze and for Christ's sake catch some fish. One of Scotty's cats must be havin' a birthday.'

Smooth dark ridges cleaved from the bow of the canoe as they paddled high up the river. The dead arms of fallen trees reached at them through the dark water. The bow ground into the coarse sand of the beach and they set up a camp on a clearing of grass beneath the blackwoods. Smoke curled in slow skeins above the tent, and Cobber's line scythed the water. He gave little grunts as he hauled it in hand over hand. 'Four pounds,' he said, holding the bream up to Mary. 'Just what we need, another fish to clean,' she smiled. 'Least it's not a flathead.'

That night they lay in the tent, listening to mullet slap the dark water and glider possums yapping in the trees. The air was drunk with pittosporum perfume. Their hands slipped along the curves of each other's bodies, smoothed the hair from the brows, touched the cheeks that glowed from the ruby gleam of the fire. And Cobber spoke of love. Talked of living like this forever. If he hadn't been so engrossed with the sound of his words in the bush, the strangeness of these words spilling off his tongue, he might have noticed her close her mouth on a laugh. Bite off derision with her teeth.

He conjured up houses and gardens, all the rich, warm things capable of being shared. She raised herself on an elbow, and her breast plumped towards his face, bed warm. She drew the covers across her chest, better to say these words.

'Listen, Cobber,' hesitating over a name that was not a name, 'this has been marvellous.' She swallowed on the inept phrases. Cobber lay still, awaiting the axe. She grabbed his jaw. 'Don't make me say silly things. I don't want to talk about all this,' and her arm swept to encompass the river and came back to restrain her breast. 'I don't jump into strange canoes for nothing. I loved Bill, still love the bastard, but I couldn't live with him and we cut each other with unforgivable words.'

34

He looked like he might talk so she pushed his chest. 'I'm going away. I'm sick of these little town lives.' She paused and traced his jaw. 'I don't want to hurt you.' Grimaced again at words that were like stones under the tongue. 'I just want to go away. I don't know what I want. Just away.'

The frail nylon of the tent had captured a bird, and Cobber watched in horror, scared that it might beat its wings against the bars until blood flecked beak and breast.

Bill passed his hand across Cathy's breast. 'I wish you'd fuck me sometimes, Bill.' Her voice startled him. He turned towards her face before he realized her intention. 'She left you Bill. Years ago. And you know she's on with Cobber.' He dropped his eyes away from her face and was stepping out of the bed. She watched his back knowing that her anger was making her voice sharp.

'I'll clean your fucking hotel rooms, Bill, I'll fuck you,' her voice was on a steep rise, her hair curling around her face in anger, panic, loss. 'I'll fuck you, but for Christ's sake fuck me, not that bloody black haired . . .' The last word was swallowed by a gasp of breath as she plunged her face into the pillow.

Bill unlocked the door to the bar and took down a bottle of Tullamore Dew and steadied his hand with the smokey liquor, rejuvenated his visions, patched up his hope. Savoured the whisky and tried to make his heart stop slamming at his ribs.

His image was returned to him from the window, black with the mask of night. He saw the shape of the man, the eyes, the hands, saw the man slouched on a stool in the court of his small kingdom. Too much travelling he thought. Too much tearing up of roots. He had followed every whim that caused her to tear up their trappings of place. Left jobs he'd enjoyed, friends that were easy, towns that had the sun of his childhood in their streets.

The grey cat walked along the bar towards him and arched

its back against his elbow. His hand curved along its back to the base of its tail. It mewed at him. Made eyes at his face.

Buying the hotel was like casting out an anchor into deep water. He waited for it to catch a rock, but she had still wanted deeper water, longed to be terrified by the sharks of experience, that gloomy underworld of the sea where the strange, large-eyed sunless beasts of the soul fought each other in the dark. On days like that she played music on the piano that made his hair rise on the back of his neck. A cat in front of a snake. The cat would always make a face and walk away on tall legs, back arched, a pretence of aggression, thinking immediately of a warm hearth.

Mary had left a note for him under the door before she left to go fishing with Cobber. 'Going away,' the note had said. The lure of more deep water. Bored with the shoal fish.


'You,' she said, opening the door.

'Me,' he said, entering. She poured drinks and passed one to him where he sat awkwardly on the edge of the couch.

'Relax, you big bastard. You make me feel sick the way you mope about when you come here. What d'you want? To annoy me? Try to drag up some guilt? Well, you can't. I'm going away and I'm not going to be –' She found his eyes on her. 'Jesus, Bill stop looking at me!' He shifted his hands and stood up, then sat in another chair.

'You don't really put me at ease, either. Look, Mary, I don't want you to go. I'm not asking you to live with me again, but I can't rip things up and follow –'

'I'm not bloody asking you to. I don't care what you do, you can – I don't mean that, but don't think I want you to come with me.'

'All right, all right. You're going, I'm staying, but just tell me where you are. What about Cobber?'

'Cobber's not coming. I don't want a man tagging along. I'll

let you know where I'm staying, Bill, I always have, haven't I?'
    'Yeah, always.'


She poured more wine
    'Come out on the verandah.' She plucked at his sleeve with
finger and thumb. He followed, but tried to keep the spaniel
out of his steps.
    Leaning against the rail, they both breathed more easily, the
scent of the pittosporum like a thick drug in their lungs. At
this time of year it was like a sleeping draught for the whole
town. She rubbed at the knuckle of his wrist.
    'One town, one house, one life after another, that's me, Bill.
And this time I'm not coming back or letting you catch up.
Each time I just feel cheated, and you feel – what do you feel?'
Her hand left his wrist, went for the glass.
    'I feel tired,' he said. 'Too many wrenches, too many turns
in the road. The new places don't thrill me like they do you. I
don't think I can change places again. I know I can't keep you
here, I don't want to. It never worked before – my wanting.
But darling –' His hand reached for her shoulder, but she drew
it away, and he dropped his arm and grasped the rail. 'I don't
know if I can stay without you.'
    'Well, we can't keep doing laps of Australia. Not together. I
can't stand the responsibility – going back to the pound to
pick up the lost dog. Let me go this time, Bill, don't try and
find me.'
    The shadows of trees slashed at the windscreen as he drove
back through the moon-bright forest. In the glass he could see
the ghost of his face lit green from the dashboard.
    He ground his teeth and wrung the steering wheel, imagin-
ing her away, being hurt, beyond his care. But he'd never kept
her from hurt under his own roof. Despite his care, love. He
didn't know about love. Couldn't imagine how it might work,
without her.

He opened the door of the chill room, and his hands dragged out the meat and vegetables for Cobber to cut up tomorrow. He ran a hand along the cool tin of the workbench, the sunken centre of the chopping block. Places he knew. Too many places.

Carlo and Cobber put her case on the bus when it pulled up at the service station. She punched Carlo softly on the chest, crushed her mouth against Cobber's lips and glanced once at the hotel before becoming a face at a window. Blue exhaust smoke swirled around them as the bus lumbered across the bridge and ground through its gears up the hills and out of the valley. Cobber listened to the fading motor of the climbing bus, wondered if the face looking from the window could see freedom, wondered if he would. He felt as if everyone was lashed to the one maypole, trying to make it bearable with gay streamers and songs. The dance of the tethered.

He fired up the huge wood stove and pushed pans of water on the hot plates. He slid dishes into the warming oven and opened the cool-room door to get out the vegetables.

Carlo was big and strong and huge bits of dirt flew from his shovel, but Scotty held up his hands and made noises with his tongue. He sliced his shovel down the sides of the hole. He looked up and moved his hand smoothly. His face quiet, the serenity of the dumb. See, he seemed to say, like this, gently, neatly. A good hole. We need a good hole.

Cobber shovelled, watching the way Scotty dug. The dumb man smiled and tapped Cobber's breastbone. Good. They smiled and dug through sand, gravel and eventually clay. Deep into the sour, yellow clay. Carlo pulled his shirt tails out and swabbed his face and neck as he stood above them at the head of the grave. 'She shouldn't have gone,' he said and jammed

his shovel into the heap of clay. 'There's nothing else up
there.' Scotty looked first at Cobber's face and then at Carlo
who was vaguely indicating a general direction for Sydney.
'Nowhere's better than here. She shouldn't have gone,' he
muttered as they watched Scotty clean up the sides.

The three of them looked into the pit. Noticed their
handiwork. Cobber was proud that he had shared the work.
Scotty was a hard task master. Demanded a good grave for a
friend. Their friend. Carlo had tears on his face.

'All right,' he bellowed, 'I cry. I cry. All right, I cry for my
good friend. I cry for that lovely girl. I cry for Scotty. I cry for
you, you silly woman-loving bastard.' He was yelling, and
Scotty held his arm and tapped Carlo's breastbone and
indicated the other headstones.

'Okay. Okay, Scotty, you mad Christian. No more noise. No
more tears.' They watched as Scotty made the sign over their
grave. The grave they had shared.

They couldn't contact her for the funeral but rang the Sydney
police. Months passed and Cobber still dreamt of faces at
windows and birds fluttering against glass; their breasts
brilliant with blood. Caged robins.

One day the bus came down the hill and as Carlo pumped
the fuel he saw the face at the window as she reached for a
case. He threw his arms around her, one hand still holding the
petrol pump. He was still muttering, 'Silly, silly girl' as the bus
heaved itself back onto the highway.

Cobber saw her by the grave and stood in the stubble waiting.
She looked up and waved, and he walked over to her. 'And I
was trying not to hurt people,' she said and quickly glanced at
his face and led him back to the gate.

'How was Sydney?' he asked at last.

'Bit like here. Probably more houses.' He didn't laugh. Neither did she. She found the flowers in her hand that she'd meant to put on the grave.

'Well, why are you back?' He wanted to know. Jealous of her other world. She glanced at him. A hard look. Still a boy.

'Perhaps I don't like a lot of houses,' she said looking down at the bouquet of boronia and thryptomene. She tossed her head back and looked at him defiantly. A savage hawk. 'And besides, I'm pregnant. I am a fish wife after all.'

# HAROLD'S TRUDY

*S*he stepped down from the bus and squinted at the sun as she walked across to the hotel, tottering slightly, high heels treacherous on the rubbly gravel. She was aware of the bus driver's eyes as he refuelled the bus. The cows and dogs and dust gave a slumbrous air to the afternoon.

The hotel was cool, and she slipped onto a bar stool and probed with her red-tipped fingers in the bag she carried. The men in the bar took in the length of her legs, her pretty knees, the hard lines around the mouth, the slight bosom; and then turned to sip the froth from their beer. The publican let his gaze travel down her body, noticing everything in the way of a man whose livelihood it is to study people.

'It's a nice day.' She looked up from her gin, where her lips had imprinted a dull red smudge on the glass. One of the men in the bar was talking to her. She nodded to him and agreed it was a nice day (as long as you like it hot and dusty).

'I expect the bus trip is tiring. All the way from Melbourne, are you?' The barman wiped glasses with his back to the bar; the other men seemed absorbed in the frost on their glasses or the texture of the bar towels. The first man spoke again to the woman.

41

'Yes, yes, it is tiring,' she said and re-crossed her legs. The eyes studying beer mats or glasses missed nothing of that eloquent action. She was aware of their eye-averted, ear-alerted attention, but she turned to the man speaking to her. She noticed the huge work-calloused hands, the clean, white shirt, the dark blue jacket and pants, clean shoes, the open, honest face, the steady, considerate eyes.

'On your way to Sydney, are you?' She watched his eyes and couldn't see in them any of the lewd prying that stalked behind the eyes of the other men and the listening back of the barman.

'Yes, I'm going to Sydney . . . to see my mother. She's sick.' One of the men coughed, and she stared coldly at him, but he didn't look up.

'Not a bad town, Sydney. Last time I was up there they were just finishing the bridge; we were just home from the war then. It was good to see the bridge as we came in through the Heads.' In the silence they all took a sip from their glasses, the barman continued to wipe the bottles, his back to the bar.

'While we waited for the train back to Melbourne, we took a trip up into the Blue Mountains. Some of the prettiest country I've ever seen, I think.' She noticed how he enunciated every word. So careful, so slow. There was no public-school clip to the speech, such as some men had affected, it was just a careful deliberation over each word, a studied but genuine politeness. He was like a child who is taught to speak politely and takes genuine pleasure in doing so. He considered it was a natural right of people to be spoken to with tact and respect.

'I've never been to the Blue Mountains, but I've heard that it's very nice up there.' She stripped a note from her purse and prepared to buy another gin.

'No, please, let me buy another drink,' and he put a note on the bar. The man in the corner coughed again, and another hid a smile behind his handkerchief as he pretended to wipe his nose. She stared at both men with her cold eyes. Neither man met her gaze.

The barman put the drinks before them.

'Thank you very much,' she said and lifted her glass to her lips.

'Here's to a safe trip to Sydney.' She took the glass away from her lips, raised it and nodded in toast, and they drank together. She could see the bus pulling out of the service station and, when she put her drink back on the bar, she knew that the barman had caught her glance at the departing bus.

She jumped up and ran to the door of the hotel.

'Oh, I've missed the bus!' She watched as it disappeared over the bridge. The barman looked at her.

'Bad luck missing the bus like that. I suppose you'll want to ring your Mum.' They stared at each other.

'Yes, I'll have to, she might worry.' The publican showed her the phone at the end of the bar.

'You can use this if you like.' He caught her glare and smiled bleakly as he pushed the phone towards her. She turned her back modestly and placed her bag by the phone so that they couldn't see her holding down the lever. She dialled some numbers and held a conversation in a low voice. She released the catch and replaced the handset.

'That'll be five shillings, miss. Costs a lot to ring Sydney.' She glared at him openly this time as he scooped the coins, his smile an ugly grimace.

'The next bus won't be through until next week, but you'll probably find plenty to do around here; it's a small town but friendly enough.' They looked at each other, understanding exactly the type of person behind the eyes.

The man who bought her the drink had turned away while she made the phone call and now turned towards her again.

'Well, if you're going to be here a while, Miss, we had better all know each other. That is Mick Tanner in the corner, Frank Cousins, Jimmy Truman, our host is Percy Miller, and I'm Harold Cottrell.' She nodded to the men, and they grunted in her direction.

'I'm Trudy Smith.' The man coughed again, and she glared

at him fiercely. She felt the barman wink behind her back and turned to stare at him, but his gaze was concentrated on polishing a glass.

As the summer afternoon became a dusk, hazy with a sinking sun and the dust from herds of milking cows ambling down the lanes, Harold and Trudy retired to the lounge to have a pub tea, heavy with potatoes and roasted meat. The other men smirked above their glasses as the publican nodded towards the lounge and winked at the men.

'That's a pro if ever I've seen one, and I'd like to have a few quid that there's no mother in Sydney. Probably going up for a job interview.' The other men laughed and discussed the woman and the gullibility of Harold. Nice legs, pity about the face; all the same, with a bag over the head, you don't look at the mantelpiece when you're stoking the fire.

When the bus came the following week Trudy was not there to meet it; she was feeding the chickens in the yard behind Harold's house. She made herself a cup of tea on the wood stove, then cradled the cup in her hands as she sat on the verandah and looked across the river to the forest where she could hear Harold's hammer wedging fence posts out of the felled trees.

The sunshine made the world seem vast and kind. The cows were gentle and they grazed in front of her or lay in the clover chewing cud with their heads rocking and eyes half closed. The chickens were like little white fluttering flags as they pecked and scratched in the leaves and bark at the edge of the clearing.

Trudy touched the gaunt skin of her face and the hard lines around her eyes and mouth. The face, she knew, would always appear hard chiselled, but a softness was there now, a relaxation of the jaw muscles.

She felt lazy and content and went inside to pour another cup of tea and cut a slice of the blackberry pie she had watched Harold make. She had asked him questions about the pastry and boiling the berries and now tasting that sharp fruit she remembered the Sunday when they had picked them.

A rabbit had bolted from the blackberry patch, and Harold threw a piece of wood and knocked it to the ground. She was not the sort of woman to cry over a dead rabbit or to wince when Harold snapped the neck to the side.

She wondered at this man, his careful polite speech, his gentleness as he held the rabbit toward her, and she had wondered at herself as she stroked the dead animal behind the ears and how Harold had bent and kissed the top of her head. She had been amazed that a man could be so gentle, that he should show so much reserve. He turned his back when they undressed at night, and when they were under the heavy possum skin rug he would spend a long time just smoothing her hair.

Used to more sudden, blunter entries into her love, she found herself almost impatient with his quiet care and deliberation. It was hard for her not to set her jaw and he noticed this, and sometimes stroked her brow and shoulders until she slept. She had watched him quiet horses or a pregnant bitch in the same way, the huge gentle hands and crooning voice stilling the trembling skin.

She looked across the river, and the donk-donk-donk of the heavy steel hammer on the wedges echoed among the trees. She let her eyes almost close and through the thicket of her lashes the sun made a swarm of golden light. She exhaled deeply and realized that she was not going back to the city, the quick and brutal work.

Trudy and Harold became accepted. They never married, either because it never occurred to them, or because the need had long passed. Two stools in the corner of the bar were reserved for them each night, and life went on. The married women at first tried to ignore her but soon found that when a woman was having her 'troubles' or difficulty with a pregnancy, it was Trudy who knew what to do. It took her a long time to learn about chickens and baking, but there were some secret areas in which she alone had the answers.

The hard lines on her face never quite went away, her fingers always remained dyed brown from the chain of cigarettes and her appetite for whisky and beer and her ability to hold them were legend. But the days and years took on a cycle of scattered wheat and shelled peas, fish from the river, prawns from the sea.

The autumn following the big drought became one of those natural landmarks against which the succession of country events is charted. A couple of years after the big flood, people would say, or, she was born in the same year as Pearson's hayshed burnt down. A calendar of calamities.

In the 'big flood' nearly all the bridges were washed down, sluggish water crept into the paddocks, slapped at farmhouse steps, and everyone waited for it to retreat as all the other floods had done.

Then it rained again. People sat inside drinking tea and watching the rain, incredulous. It must stop! But it didn't. Then a storm dropped sheets of water that drummed on the iron roof so hard that the entire house shook. Harold couldn't believe that it could continue and watched the filthy brown foam eddying among the crowns of trees on the river bank.

'The chooks!' Trudy called as she looked out the back window. 'And the calf, Harold, the calf is out in the water!' He noticed the tears caught in the lines around her eyes and tried to remember if he had ever seen her cry.

They were both slopping outside in the mud in slick coats, their hair flat against their skulls, water running into their eyes and mouths.

Harold reached the calf and began carrying it back to the shed. Trudy was hurrying the hens up to the cow shed away from the flood and, as they worked, they screamed to each other through the rain and the wind and the rumble of the moving water.

The tank stand was threatening to fall, and Harold propped a stay against it and turned to see Trudy breast deep in the water reaching for a chicken afloat on the stream. She grasped the chicken before it could be dashed away but tripped on something under the water, and bobbed and splashed trying to gain a foothold. She still held the chicken, but Harold could see the bulk of a tree slowly swing around.

He raced towards her, splashing across the farmyard, and heard the scream as the tree rolled across her.

'Trudy!' he yelled, and the echo came back to him from the sodden hills. 'Trudy!' He could see her dress snagged in the head of the tree, and he untied the skiff from the verandah with shaking hands and pushed it into the water, trying to follow, but it was well out and the water tumbled the tree and Harold drifted along with the current, gazing across the dirty water dimpled by the rain.

When the skiff bucked and he was thrown into the water, he seemed unaware of his plight. He stumbled to the bank and stood on a rocky knoll with a clump of sodden sheep and some frightened wallabies and rabbits. He watched the logs and bloated cows bobbing past and when it became too dark to see he sat with his back to a tree.

The rain stopped and the floods receded, exposing the grass and piles of debris, huge trees and tangles of fences, stinking, swollen cows and oil drums. And a body. Held fast in the fork of limbs, Trudy became visible as the water lapped at the tree, her hair and dress spread out on water the colour of stewed and milky tea.

Harold didn't say much again. At the funeral the sun shone and the flood had gone, but the ground was still making quiet seeping sounds as water drained through the soil. Harold didn't pay much attention to the funeral and returned home to sit on the verandah and watch the fence posts begin to re-appear beside the river. So the mason chipped in the legend on a piece of local granite.

# NIGHT ANIMALS

No one knew if Harold visited the grave. He spent each day looking out across the river to the hills where he used to cut sleepers and fence posts.

A neighbour called in every now and then with a pot of soup or stew, and Harold would thank her in his careful voice.

One day another granite stone appeared beside Trudy's. Before funerals the weeds were pulled away from headstones and the little pickets straightened and the local men toiled to sink the shaft into clay.

Some famous explorer and grazier was laid in that cemetery and from time to time a tourist bus would pull up, and for a few minutes the people would stand around the impressive slab and monument in the centre of the cemetery plot. They would photograph the plaque and each other and then step gingerly through the long grass to proceed to the next historic landmark, canoe tree, famous building, another cemetery.

Sometimes a restless child or bored woman would wander away from the group and part the seeding grass heads from the faces of two headstones and wonder about Harold Cottrell and his Trudy.

Then they would light a cigarette or unwrap another lolly and wander back to the bus and it would grind its gears, heading for the next great moment in history.

# CICADAS

*T*here was no hint in the dust. The runes left by snakes and lizards and smaller aimless beetles held messages for the boy, but nothing to make him aware of what he was to find. There was nothing in the magpie's song, or the steady gaze of kangaroos to tell him that anything more unusual was happening than the ponderous progress of a globe's track in space. To the boy it was hot because it was summer, and summer meant cicadas. He held the transparent amber case of one that had crawled from the earth, cast off its shell, sung its song and died. Enough awe for a boy in one day.

In his other hand he held a bundle of letters for a man his father said was crazy, and if his father said a man was crazy then that man was. In the boy's mind, any man who could fix tractors also had the authority to judge the life of another man. Still, it was the boy's job to carry the mail from his father's farm the two miles along the track to old Joe Freeman's hut. His father said that Joe might be crazy, bush crazy, but he was still a good bloke, who did no harm, worked hard and had to be treated with respect.

The boy cared nothing for the letters, even the stamps he gave only a glance. He poked among a pile of old cans and bottles he had poked among every time he had walked this track. He opened the door of the rusty oven as he had done every time and inspected it for funnel webs or bush mice, but there was nothing. He slammed the door, and it did not occur to him that he trampled among the rusting and shattered dreams of some unknown man's passion.

At last he came upon the wattle clearing where Joe's hut stood, and the goanna near the door meant nothing except the almost irresistible urge to throw a stone at the ugly hissing monster, but this was another man's property, and his father said throwing stones on another man's land was not to be done.

The door of the hut was open, and Joe was sitting in his chair cleaning his rifle, and the boy's foot was on the step and his mouth already open to greet the man until he smelt it and saw it in the eye and then he noticed the patch under the chin, and his gaze travelled in an eternity of cicada-shrilled time away from the face and down to the hand which wasn't quite holding the barrel.

Each night after that his mind reeled in a slow agonizing gaze down the length of barrel to the hand locked in a claw on the trigger, and then he would be flung sweating into consciousness by a single blast. Boyhood was invaded by the troubles which cause all the bland and freckled foreheads to corrugate and the corners of vacant eyes to develop a permanent squint of suspicion as boys turn to men and regard the sun with wonder and a dark hint of dread.

A man sat at a plain table with his back to the door. A woman holding a teapot regarded the man in silence, a hesitant, appealing look which struggled with exasperation. She stirred at last and poured tea for Joe Freeman. Could any man be so silent, could any man sit so stiffly in new, ill-fitting clothes, could any man look up into a woman's eyes with so much love? She glanced at him across her cup but snatched her eyes away and bit her lip and would have bitten it through, such was her anger that he should cause her to feel this way. She struggled to control a shudder at the look of dog devotion in those eyes.

Their cups rattled in the silence, and he didn't hear the imperceptible tremble of her indrawn breath, but he saw the rise of her chest and knew she would speak.

'Tell me, Joe, why is it that you travel for two days by horse and train to sit here and say nothing?' He drank before he spoke, his cracked and strained hands clasping the cup. His eyes, full of a dark flame, fixed hers.

'Because I love you,' and he held her eyes with his gaze. His hands tightened around the cup. 'Because I'd do anything for you. Because the only thing I care about is you, always have done and always will, and you know it.' His hand plunged forward, released by a gush of words, and grasped hers. Their eyes struggled and at last her arms were around him, her breasts against him. Her lips trembled at his neck for a moment and then were gone like a moth that flutters against a lamp-lit window for a second and then, on powdery wings, seeks another lit casement in all that billowing pitch of night.

Her face was against his shoulder, and he breathed in the sweet liquor of her hair, his head swimming in that vapour of warm woman flesh. He could feel her woodenness in his arms. They were standing on her balcony which looked down into the creek and across the hills to the sea which surged in the night like a muffled heart. At last she turned from him to look out across the creek, and he too turned stiffly and clutched the balcony rail, looking at the lights of Sydney winking through trees on the edge of the harbour; looking through eyes misted with a passion that threatened to split his heart and strangle him with the cords of his own neck.

'Joe,' she said, 'I can't give what you ask.' She looked into his face beseeching his eyes to understand that she didn't want to hurt or be hurt, meant no harm to him. 'Joe, I'm just not ready for that, perhaps never will be. Every time you come I feel dread, because you ask me for something I'm not willing to give, perhaps not even able to give.' There was a silence in the night, and she found more words. 'I know you say nothing, but all the time you put a weight on my heart. I don't want to be held down, I want – ' Her clenched eyes stared into the night but couldn't find what she wanted.

His hand went to her shoulder and he allowed himself the luxury of slipping his fingers inside the fall of her hair to caress the soft skin behind her ear, and he knew that his fingers would feel it forever and his neck would never cease to cringe with sudden desire each time he remembered her breath against him.

'I'm going back in the morning, but you must know I want no other woman,' and he looked at where he had drawn back her hair from her neck. 'No one will ever mean what you mean to me,' and he bent down and placed his lips gently upon hers, aware that she struggled not to turn away. The night enfolded them, the surf beat in them, her heart was the shore trembling to the wave overpeaked with its own power, crashing like a huge tree to the ground.

At last she said in a voice edged with exasperation, 'You can sleep in my bed. There's no other except the couch, but that's hard, and there's no need.' She kissed him quickly on the cheek and was gone. He stood for a long time on the balcony and at last turned into the house, undressed and lay down beside her. Both lay rigidly, he aching to let his hand caress the curve of her breast and hip, she gritting her teeth, hoping he wouldn't.

The silence surged on, and at last he felt that she relaxed at the threshold of sleep, and his face was inches from the lush mesh of her hair. His hand was upon her arm and slid to her waist, cradled the hip and at last felt the warmth of her belly, and his eyes swam, the world overheeled as his hand cupped her breast. He lay with his head thrown back, a huge surf beating behind his eyes, across his chest, swamping his loins. She held his hand to her breast for a moment and then gently took it and placed it on her waist. She was soon asleep, and all night he listened to her breathing and his breathing, and towards morning she turned in her sleep and he shifted his face into the path of her breath and, as dawn came, he took in her air and watched her face, her eyes like a child's, the mouth open, the freckles around her neck vulnerable in their childishness.

When she opened her eyes, they met his, and she felt her hand holding his arm. The planet turned on its axis a moment before she groaned and stretched in the languor of warm sleep. Nothing in the world would have prevented him from taking her in his arms and loving her, feeling himself in herself, nothing at all, except that she didn't want it, and he couldn't bear the look of reproach he imagined she would give. For all the huge force of blood that was in him, it could be quelled by one look of her eyes. She was not a cold woman, had he not slept by her side and felt the unbearable lushness and richness of her; it was just that she was withheld.

With thick fingers he prepared a pot of tea while she made toast, and they allowed these preparations to consume their attention, until at last they sat opposite each other at a table, and he smiled. He remembered the girlishness of her body and smiled with love. He knew he would soon be on his way back to the forests of the mountains, but for a moment his soul blazed with love, and she looked full into his eyes and let her eyes search his eyes, but neither could prevent the blundering motion of the sphere, and the moment passed.

As he stood at her door, case in hand, the moment for the inevitable parting kiss came, and in their clumsiness their faces clashed, and their lips might have touched but it was sudden, and they drew apart. He was about to say something, and she could tell by the suddenness of the indrawn breath that it would be a farewell false with heartiness and she said instead, 'Joe, don't rush me, give me time,' and once again she pecked at his cheek and drew back to tuck the hair away from her face. He said nothing, and she could see the spanielness looming in his eyes, but he gave a quick nod and turned and as he swung the gate she said, 'Write to me,' and she could tell by his back that he heard.

He wrote long letters of his love, and she wrote back brief notes, mostly about her job and house and these were carried by trains through a blur of eucalypt forest and wild ranges. After a time the letters to Sydney took longer to be answered, and the silences in midnight forests became longer, and the agony of the sensation on his neck and palm more unbearable, and finally one morning young Bill Peterson stood in the doorway grasping the mail from Sydney and stared into the hut until at last he rushed from the doorstep, and it wasn't until half way home that he felt the letters still in his hand and flung them far into the ferns and wattles and ran in a wild-eyed rush to his father.

The letters fell among the bracken and settled with the passage of sun and rains. The rubber band blistered in the heat, and a possum flipped them over with his paw, but they smelt of nothing, and he went on. The two bills re-joined the earth after a succession of rains and suns and the ink of the other gradually ran and bleached and finally was frittered by the passage of ants until no single word could be made out, but anyway nobody passed that way.

Bill Peterson's dreams were haunted by the same ghastly track down the rifle barrel and his eyes, screwed tight during the dream, never lost the look of surprise that life should turn out like this.

The boy had gone, the man had come, but he was not quieted by the transition. Whenever he found the frail vacated shells of cicadas he would still turn them over in his hand, but now the bulging eyes made him shudder, the transparent claws clutched his fingers. The cicada had emerged from the chrysalis to sing its song.

# *SPLITTER*

*T*o the magpie at the top of a dead wattle, he was just a man with his dog.

The man woke slowly, rubbing his cheek against the trunk of the tree, and the magpie cocked his head the other way, looked for a moment and then carolled the warbling, rolling, sun bursting song of the morning; sang it to the clear beads held in the fronds of ferns and to the yellow and pink glow of the sunrise through the trees.

To the man, as he awoke, the song of the magpie reminded him of the morning on the road to Berwick. The morning where he awoke with black-eyed, long-lashed jerseys blinking slowly at him and rolling cud between their jaws.

The morning after leaving Melbourne and home. On the road for work. He remembered the Salvos had given him a bowl of soup while he waited in the dole queue, and he had listened to the other men talking of jobs that might come up or places where you could get a feed. Other men said nothing at all but tried to hide the soles of their shoes or pretend they wore a shirt beneath their coat. Two had talked about cutting railway sleepers in the hills around Erica and Orbost.

Ah, now he remembered where he was, and he looked up to

see the magpie watching him. Now he was fully, bare daylight awake, and he looked down at his left arm where it disappeared into the side of the log. The reality he had hoped would turn out to be a dream.

He looked at his dog, slowly beating its tail in the forest litter and whining. The man turned his eyes to the axe ten feet away and the signs of six days' struggle in trying to reach it. His tongue ran across his lips, and he looked at the sky where the best of the sunrise yellow was being blanched from the horizon by a furnacing summer day. Slowly, he dropped his face to the log and licked at the wood alcohol mixed with the dew and once more sank into unconsciousness.

A blurred image of a suburban back garden with honeysuckle and a huge peach tree. A young girl under the tree playing jacks with knuckle bones, elbow deep in soap suds, tangled hair falling about her tight-lipped face. And then a dog appeared, a pup, a black and white kelpie cross. The pup was growling and chewing a stick.

Once again the man blinked into consciousness and the images disappeared. Not far away a black and white dog was whining gently and beating the dust and twigs with his slowly wagging tail. As he saw the man's eyes open, the dog clawed at the ground in front of him and made as if to rush towards his master but sat up and continued his tail beating and whining. The man stared at the dog as reality clubbed his brain – like the back of an axe. Ah, the axe, and his eyes wandered once again to his axe. He pushed his boot a few inches towards the axe but stopped. These last six days it hadn't reached, why should it reach today. He pushed at his leg anyway, but the boot seemed heavier, and he didn't seem able to bend his knee. He gave up and slewed his eyes to his arm. He ran his black swollen tongue across his lips and bent to lick at the log, but its dew had long since dried, and the taste of sap nauseated him, and his stomach felt like a dried pea cringing in the huge cave of his chest.

He pulled his arm, but of course it wouldn't move, and he

could still feel the steel wedge beneath his crushed hand.

He opened his mouth to call the dog over, but the dog just clawed at the ground, and his throat could utter no sound. The fingers of his free hand searched beneath the log for leaves he had missed or a worm or beetle that had strayed there since his last search. But there was nothing.

The dog whined and scratched deeper into the flinty ground. How many times had he called the dog to fetch the axe and how many times had the dog brought back sticks only to be sent away. And in his frustration and misery the dog bit at the trees and clawed at the ground but could not understand.

The free hand slowly crept up to the tear in the shirt and resumed a clawing at the shoulder of the trapped arm. His fingers dragged at his flesh, but the wound was changing colour, and the pain only brought the relief of unconsciousness as the blood beat behind his eyes. Blackness slugged his mind, and his forehead fell with a crack against the log. The hand dropped away from his shoulder, the nails clogged with his own flesh and blood.

In the flickery newsreel of his dream the hand reached into the split log to retrieve the wedge and then, frame by frame, the wedge spun clear, and his mind watched as time telescoped and the log slowly closed upon his arm even while he tried to snatch it out. In the dream his shoulder twitched as he begged the muscles to beat the end of the film. But they never did.

When O'Byrne no longer came to pick up tea and sugar at the Cabbage Tree store, and when timber fellers no longer saw smoke rising from his chimney and when his pile of box sleepers did not increase it was no surprise to anyone. Splitters were in the bush for weeks at a time on their own, and O'Byrne was a queer sort at the best of times. In these restless years, men would often up and leave and never be seen again. That summer, O'Byrne was not a topic of conversation at all. A few farmers in the hills talked of a wild black dog raiding the chicken pens, but it was desultory talk. There were many such dogs in the bush and besides the heat of this incredible summer and the threat of fire were on everyone's mind.

Years later, a cutter clambered up from the fern gully and came to a pile of sleepers and a billy can by an old fire. He walked further into the clearing, and a black dog rushed at him and stood snarling, his yellow teeth bared beneath quivering lips. The cutter saw the skeleton and the bones of the forearm caught in the split log. With one eye on the dog, the man cast about the clearing and saw the wedge on the ground where it had sprung from the log and guessed that the hand that belonged to this bleached bone probably gripped a second wedge. The tree had closed on the man who would have split it, and the dog who would have saved him had watched him die and now desperately tried to protect an ever decreasing pile of bones from the ravages of fire, goannas and eventually, another man.

# THE SLAUGHTERS OF THE BULUMWAAL BUTCHER

*B*odies had always been found. Dogs, kangaroos, sometimes even cattle and horses had been found, dreadfully mutilated, the heads torn completely from the bodies.

This was Nargun country, and the Aborigines said that these slaughters had been occurring far back in black memory and were attributed to the Nargun, the stone beast which on some still, frosty nights roamed through the hills looking for food.

The white population claimed that an escaped panther from a travelling circus was the culprit; others thought that a Yowie was responsible. Old Clive Glossop, the post splitter, reckoned he had seen a huge hairy beast massacre a big kangaroo in his paddock. The pile of Ruby port bottles outside his shack was enough evidence for most people to discredit this story.

It's true that old Mrs Muir disappeared without trace ten years ago, leaving the kettle on the stove and the radio tuned to 'Evening Concert', and it's also true that Murphy's huge Friesian cow gave birth to an extraordinarily ugly hairy calf; but all of these thing were classified by most people as those mysterious affairs that occur, but which have perfectly simple scientific explanations. Mrs Muir could have fallen down a mine shaft, and Murphy's cow probably just had a freak calf. And Glossop – well, everybody knew about Clive Glossop.

But this was a bit different. Since the start of winter over twenty sheep had been killed. Their heads were torn from their bodies, and the guts and feet found strewn in their clotted blood. The manner of the deaths was similar to the mutilations of the kangaroos and dogs. Perc Hopkins, the Aboriginal rouseabout from the saw mill, saw one of the sheep and began grumbling about Narguns and pointed up into the hills where a huge granite tor stood out in the open pasture. That was the Nargun, Perc claimed, and any night he might wake up and come looking for tucker.

Although Perc immediately took his first holiday in thirty years and went to visit his cousins on the Murray, the whites still talked about some logical explanation, like an escaped panther or a Tasmanian Tiger. Clive Glossop insisted on his Yowie story, but he was given two bottles of Ruby port and sent home.

The massacre of sheep continued during the winter, and over the Sunday roast Les Patterson told his wife it was about time something was done. Les, a shire councillor and football club president, went to the pub on the following night and there he met Clarrie Watson, Dan Murphy and Tom Mullins, sheep farmers all. Little Phonce Wallace-Pimble, the chemist and Bulumwaal councillor, was also there, and so a meeting was held, and they determined that they would find the sheep killer and put a stop to this nonsense about Yowies, panthers and Narguns. The council had always held the responsibility for quelling civic imagination.

A week later this same group of solid citizens stood around the latest scene of massacre and counted the heads and remains of eleven sheep. Les pointed out the tyre marks in the mud a hundred yards down the track. Ten days later they stood looking down at the remains of more sheep scattered in the frosty grass.

Phonce Wallace-Pimble was short of breath in the crispness

of the morning, and his face was wreathed in vapour as he ventured that this carnage might be the work of wild dogs and dingoes.

Les Patterson looked down at the little chemist and smoke seemed to snort from his nostrils as he declared such talk to be nonsense. Later he told Tom Mullins that he couldn't expect anything more sensible from a town man who didn't have the good sense to wear decent boots when walking around in frosty paddocks.

Les didn't miss the tyre tracks in the soft soil near the paddock gate, and later that day stood behind Jack Slattery's truck and recognized the same tread. Les rubbed his chin and went to the hotel. He leant on the bar as the others spouted their theories over foaming pots. Narguns, panthers, and Yowies were favoured possibilities, but wild dogs were, as always, clear favourites. Some farmers would have blamed wombats, koalas and corellas if they hadn't been vegetarians.

As the slaughters continued, the more bizarre and frightening theories gained credence. Herb Nash, the local alcoholic and wit, was scared of nothing, but suggested it could be the work of Mrs Kestrel, the local school mistress and witch. This became a popular theory among children: bloody sheep feet began to appear on the teacher's table, and mysterious bleatings would issue from a class of students who appeared to be working harder than they ever had before.

The story of the ram being let loose in the school house seemed a great joke and, in the hotel that night, the story went through many stages of elaboration, including wild exaggerations of the various delights and frights experienced by either the ram or Mrs Kestrel. That the school mistress's bloomers had been rent by the ram's horns could not be doubted because Les Patterson had seen them himself when he went to retrieve his stud ram. As a councillor his word could not be doubted and when he said he would kill the kid who kidnapped his ram, that was not doubted either, and several kids immediately went down with apparently incurable cases of flu, dysentery and fits.

It didn't seem quite so funny the next morning when the cleaner found Mrs Kestrel hanging from the school bell with a note addressed to her sister propped on the desk where all her papers and books had been carefully packed away. She had chalked a 'No School Today' notice on the board and left enough spelling and maths to last two weeks. It was considered by many rather unfortunate in retrospect that the words 'you, yew and ewe' had been included. Among the books she had corrected the night before, police found that a student, beside the poem 'Baa baa, black sheep', had chosen to illustrate it with a picture of a witch and a huge cauldron of dismembered sheep. Mrs Kestrel had begun to write the usual good work legend but had apparently stopped on seeing the illustration accompanying the poem. Neighbours who had heard a desultory clanging of the bell had thought the wind was responsible and had continued to watch Brian Naylor's version of the news.

Les was worried by other things. The death of the schoolteacher was the result of an unfortunate town prank, although he had harboured suspicions about the school mistress since he himself had been a child at the school. Mrs Kestrel had kept him in on one occasion and blasted him with tongue and cane, and he never forgot her piercing eyes and wicked laugh and the way her neck and face flushed with excitement as she beat and harangued her victim.

But Les knew she had not been responsible for the sheep. He also knew Jack Slattery, and Jack was a close friend, a solid citizen and a fellow member of the Chamber of Commerce. Times were becoming hard for graziers, and the whole district was suffering a prolonged recession. The export of stud rams had made an impact on traditional markets for Australian lamb, and many farmers, including Les, were mortgaged several times over.

Les decided that a visit to Jack Slattery was vital. Jack was curious when Les ignored his wife, the good Edith Slattery, and

62

asked for a private talk. Jack was a genial man and thought that Les had found an excuse for the two of them to share a few beers and discuss the latest intrigues in the process of syphoning money away from the pre-school and elderly citizens' funds in order to seal certain access roads to rural properties.

Jack hurried to get cans and chips so that they could get down to tintacks. Les looked uncomfortable and finally said, 'Ar, look, Jack, it's about these sheep.' Jack began pouring beer into glasses with manic concentration.

'What sheep?' he said, apparently uninterested.

'Now come on, Jack, we've been mates for a long time. You know bloody well what sheep.' Jack was short, tubby, red-faced, bristly about nose and ears, but glassily clean shaven elsewhere. Les, lean and weathered with pale grey, penetrating eyes, regarded his friend with impatient discomfort. He was used to the dumb predictability of sheep, dogs and councillors, and this sophistry was making it difficult for him to find a comfortable position in his chair.

'Look, Jack, don't play possum with me. There's been over thirty sheep killed recently, and I've seen your tyre treads at the scene of every – well, every – slaughter.' The word was hard for Les to say, and he took a deep draught of beer.

The local butcher looked carefully at his angular friend, and his mind tried to assess the possibility of subterfuge, but then he relaxed and smiled. He was as concerned as a rabbit when it is cornered by a kangaroo dog. Under such circumstances intelligence is of no use; it is a contest between the relative power of jaws and flesh. Les, Jack decided, definitely had the canines. It was time for whippet and rabbit to make a deal.

Jack explained the expense of bringing meat from Bairnsdale, the poor economic climate of the town, his own financial difficulties due to an unfortunate gamble in gold investment and how he had decided to procure cheap meat for his butchery.

'We've always been good mates, Les,' he said, and on a

sudden inspiration his pouch of brains tossed up an idea. 'Now, look, we could organize this properly. You farmer blokes are getting nothing for your sheep at the markets, and I can't compete with the big butchers, so why don't we keep the old panther scare going. We could –' He searched for details. 'We could form a syndicate of farmers and butcher our own sheep, leave the heads in the paddock and make a decent profit for a change. All we'd have to do would be to keep it quiet.' Jack and Les looked at each other.

The following evening a small group of farmers – Tom Mullins, Dan Murphy, Les Patterson, Clarrie Watson, Jack Slattery the butcher, and inevitably, despite Les's distaste for the man, Phonce Wallace-Pimble the chemist – talked over the scheme at a quiet table in the pub. A darts competition kept the other patrons engaged, and as the barman called for blokes to get their last drinks and get out, the syndicate shook hands.

The slaughters continued. The financial prospects of a few farmers improved, the butcher flourished, and the syndicate muddied the waters by shredding their sheep dogs' winter coats and fixing tufts of dog hair into the barbed-wire fences wherever a slaughter had taken place.

The wild-dog theory gained immediate credence, and syndicate members pointed at various reprobate town dogs, which were at once put to death. Les, Jack and Phonce got the council to put up vermin notices calling for the death of wild dogs, the government was approached by the shire to begin trapping dingoes, and funds were poured in by the local farmer-elected politician. Most of the money went to finish road works out to the farms of syndicate members and to provide a new awning for the chemist and butcher shops.

The dog trapper visited his traps for a fortnight without trapping or even seeing a wild dog, but the Lands Department forgot they had sent him there, and the computer kept on paying him. It seemed like a fair thing to him so he stayed on, bought a house, married the baker's daughter, failed to catch dogs, but succeeded in supporting the bar of the hotel.

The slaughters went on. Disgruntled sheep dogs had tufts of fur torn from their bodies so that it could be applied to barbed wire but, in general, rural life continued. Even the fortunes of the local footy sides picked up, and the Bulumwaal Blues registered their first win in three seasons. The butcher supplied free lamb chops to celebrate their victory.

One morning Jack Slattery and Clarrie Watson were just loading the last carcasses into the butcher's van when they saw old Clive Glossop hurrying into the bush towards his hut in the hills. Jack and Clarrie were holding the warm carcass of one of Clarrie's wethers between them, and they looked at each other. Old Clive had certainly seen them, but would anyone believe him? They quickly covered up the evidence of the slaughter and didn't even knot dog fur into the barbed wire.

That night in the hotel the syndicate met and digested the news that Jack and Clarrie brought to the meeting. The bar was rowdy and still incoherently celebrating the one consecutive win of the local footy team. Clarrie and Les were selectors for the team, and it was assumed that they were planning an assault on the Tabberaberra Tigers.

The syndicate could reach no decision. Their scheme was financially rewarding at a time when farmers around the continent were leaving their farms. And yet, one word from Clive Glossop, despite his reputation as an alcoholic, could cause a scandal, especially among the farmers in more desperate financial plight who had not been invited to join the Bulumwaal butchers' syndicate.

It was tentatively decided to buy off Clive with a side of lamb each month, a case of Ruby port and a generous contract for fence posts. Some of the syndicate members felt that the very inclusion of such vast quantities of Ruby port would make Clive an untrustworthy member of the party. They decided to meet the next night to discuss the matter further and in the meantime slaughters would temporarily cease.

The next night the syndicate stood silently at the bar ready to begin their meeting after a couple of quick pots to clear the head. Les put his glass down and was just about to begin when Phonce Wallace-Pimble burst in through the doors, hair dishevelled, tie askew, and eyes wild. The dart spectators stared at the little chemist, who was covering his face with tiny pink hands. The pub fell silent. The darts player stood with dart poised to throw. The barman poured beer all over his hand. The syndicate members were frozen, some in the act of finishing off the last drops of beer. Jack had a hand in his pocket ready for his shout, and Les's hand was placed on the bar in the manner of a chairman impatient to begin. All looked towards Phonce.

'It's Clive,' the chemist said, and passed an arm across his eyes. 'He's dead, he's dead, the dogs must have got him! His – his head's been torn off, and his body's gone except for the legs –' The barman came around the bar and pressed a stiff brandy into the chemist's quivering hand. Phonce drank quickly and went on. 'He'd been sick for a few days, and I ordered some medicine from Melbourne, and when I took it out to him, there he was – with this.' Phonce held up a port bottle and only Les noticed the peculiar brownish stain on the under side of Phonce's sleeve.

The syndicate members looked from one to the other, searching for the eyes of the one who had found the solution to their problem. Les looked at Phonce, and Phonce looked back. Les moved to the chemist's side and took the bottle from him and carefully lowered Phonce's upraised arm.

'Well, it looks like the dogs, all right,' said Les, and immediately the bar was full of conjectures, predictions and proposals, and more local dogs came under the scrutiny of the bar-room investigations. 'I betcha it's the bookie's Pekinese,' said a rugged gambler. Other eyes cast about the bar for dogs. The publican's black labrador, which had slept in a corner of the pub every night for fifteen years, suddenly woke up and found thirty men staring at him; he yelped once, dashed for the door, and was never seen again.

The council redoubled its efforts to raise government funds to deal with the menace, the Lands Department discovered that it still had a dog trapper in the area and immediately gave him the sack. The computer continued to pay for him for five years.

Worst of all, the sheep slaughters were repeated regularly, and on these nights many people had seen the ghost of old Clive Glossop roaming the paddocks screaming in a voice that echoed far across the moonlit paddocks, 'Butchers! butchers, butchers!'

The menace that threatened the flocks by night became known as the Bulumwaal Butcher and speculation on the form of the dread beast was both varied and bizarre. The local council had no answer to the problem, and people learned to live with the ravages of local livestock. And besides, the footy team won another game and the chemist turned on a pie night. Not such a bad bloke after all – for a chemist.

# WORK-HORSES

'Your mother's busy,' Grandpa would say to the boy as they fished in the creek. 'There's nine of you kids, and she's got no one to help her, that's why you've got to be the man of the house, Alf. You're the only one who can look after your Mum now.' He'd think for a bit and fiddle with his line. 'She's a good woman, your mother, and she loves all you kids, that's what you've got to remember. If she gives you a hidin', it's probably because you deserve two. She's not a light-hearted woman, but then light hearts are for people with nothin' heavy on 'em.' He'd pull in a blackfish. 'Three more for a feed, young Alf; 'bout time ya pulled yer weight.'

The boy loved his Grandpa and loved fishing and rabbiting with him, but most of all he loved going out to work with the old man in the cart drawn by the Clydesdales.

Grandpa Palmer's team didn't have flashy bells and plumes, just greasy leather tack and horse collars patched up with pieces out of old boots. But these horses were pulling a long dray made from deep slabs of ironbark, not some gold and green jinker for prancing around the Melbourne streets. Grandpa Palmer had work-horses.

The boy worked with his Grandpa ramming the clay hard

down against the base of fence posts and running wires along the length of the line, but his mind would often turn to his greatest joy. Hanging on the axles under the cart were two bags. One for sweet creek water, cooled by its own evaporation and the other for doorstep sandwiches and apples. If Grandpa had been killing sheep, the bread would be filled with cold lamb; if not, with rabbit they had caught together. The two of them would lean back against the cart wheels and Grandpa Palmer would dish out the tucker. He'd pass a sandwich to the boy with the same comment every day. 'Now get stuck into one of these, me boy, it'll put hairs on ya chest.' Then they'd eat the apples and have a drink out of the neck of the waterbag.

The old man always had a White Crow sauce bottle full of cold tea, which the boy would be allowed to drink when he proved he was a man. He rolled cigarettes with fingers as thick as carrots and looked at the boy as he licked the edge of the paper. 'And ya can have one of these when yer old enough to need one.' The big man would lie on his back and tip the hat over his eyes and drag deeply and blissfully while the boy breathed in the skeins of delicious smoke and listened to the horses lazily stomping feet to shake off the flies. He didn't know if he wanted to smoke, but he did know he wanted to be a man – like his grandpa. To know about horses, and fencing and catching things to bring to the table. To work.

At the end of the day they'd stand and look along the fence they had made, the beautiful singing of the wire through the waving rye grass and the good feeling in the stomach when you punched the post with the heel of your hand and it made no move.

'That's good, Alf,' the old man would say. 'You've done well. That's a post that'll never let no cow through.' Up at the farmhouse the farmer they'd been working for would carefully pour a beer for Grandpa Palmer, and the women would give the boy homemade lemonade.

The men would sip at their beers. These were not times to

gulp. As they left, the farmer would re-cap the bottle, and the boy knew that tomorrow the two men would drink from the same bottle again.

'Times are hard, Alf – awful hard.' They rode home in the dray with their pay, a bag of spuds and pumpkins. 'Could ya smell what that woman was cookin' for their tea, Alf? Turnip stew, son – turnip bloody stew – and I bet you could hold the turnips with one hand that went into it.'

The old man shook his head, and when they pulled up at the shed he unloaded the bags into the airing room and Grandma came and wiped her hands on her apron. The old man wouldn't look up.

'Pumpkins, Stan,' she said.

'Pumpkins, Else. Two days' fencing worth of pumpkins. They're cookin' turnips for their tea. 'Least we've got a few two-tooth in the paddock.' She put her hand on the old man's back and rubbed his shoulders.

'Come in and have a cuppa and a bath, Stan, and Alfie, you'll need a man's slice of bread and jam after a day's work like that.' Together the old people watched the boy as he ran to hug the sightless sheepdog on the verandah.

'He can work, Else, by Jesus he can work. Ya wouldn't reckon he could lift that bar, let alone plug clay with it.'

Back at home, he gave his mother the florin Grandpa had paid him for his work, and she stared down at it and then slipped it into the old teapot on the mantelpiece. She said nothing. It was never enough. Nine kids. What could you do?

He delivered papers from the bike he'd built out of tip parts. He got up in the dark every day and ran on the spot to keep warm while he pulled on his shirt and jumper. He crept from the room where his brothers and sisters slept and wheeled his bike out into the street, the sky becoming a dishwater grey. False dawn.

At the top of the Kew hill was a house so big that he imagined the prime minister must live there. One morning he met the man at its front gate and handed him the paper. As he took the rolled-up *Argus* the man couldn't help seeing the old socks the boy had pulled over his hands as gloves. Next day there was a woman at the gate holding a parcel out to him. 'These are for you, and this is for your Mum.' The woman hurried into the house and watched him behind the curtains as he rode away with the twin sacks of papers slung across his bike and the parcels pushed up his jumper.

After he'd finished his round he showed the parcels to his mother while she pushed cereal into his little sister's mouth.

'Where'd you get them?'

'Lady on the hill gave 'em to me. This one's for you.' She put down the spoon and unwrapped the package, and there was a leg of lamb and half a pound of bacon. The baby smacked her hand into the cereal bowl and the mush flew into the air.

'Eunice, for goodness' sake!' the mother said, and wiped up the mash as the boy unwrapped the other parcel and held up the school blazer, gloves, socks and long trousers.

His brothers and sisters stood around him as he pulled on the pants. The woman pushed her grey hair back into its combs and burst into tears. She rocked her head on the tray of the high chair, shuddering with great gulping sobs, and the baby tugged at her hair with its porridgey hands.

But nothing was enough. The leg of lamb could only last them two days, the socks had to go to young Aub and everyone shared the gloves.

At the weekend Alf stood in his grandparents' kitchen and showed them the blazer. The old man moved up close and peered at the pocket. 'Melbourne Grammar, eh?' But his grandmother walked around him smiling. 'You look lovely, Alf, real smart ya look, and remember this, Alf, it was kind of Mrs Beckwith to give you the blazer, but you earned it. Remember that, you earned it.'

Grandpa Palmer stalked out of the room and brought back a packet of square biscuits. 'That's what gave ya the blazer, me boy – Beckwith's bloody biscuits, that's who –'

'Now, Stan,' said the old woman, 'don't get Bolshy. It was

nice of Mrs Beckwith to give it to the boy, and that's that.'
Grandpa Palmer went out into the yard and chopped enough
stove logs for a month, and his grandson could hear him
growling 'Beckwith's' as he slammed the axe into each block
of stringybark.

There were more parcels. Each time there'd be a school
jumper, pants, gloves, socks, a pair of ballet shoes for the girls
(although none of them knew what ballet was) and sometimes
a piece of meat or bacon. One day he brought home another
parcel with another pair of long pants in it, and the other kids
gathered around as he gave them to his younger brother.

'Now don't tear the bloody things, Aub, or I'll wring ya
bloody neck. I – I earned them.' The woman came in from
washing the clothes and saw her children gathered round her
son in his new pants.

She didn't cry. She just hung the clothes basket back on the
hook and breathed to herself, 'Beckwith's, and not a biscuit in
the place.'

Eventually Aub took over the paper round and received the
gifts from Beckwiths, while Alf went into an apprenticeship.
Still his solace was to work beside his grandmother, freed
from the responsibilities of his own home.

But even here he found the work falling more heavily in his
hands. If they carried something between them, Alf noticed
how he got the heavy end. More and more, Grandpa Palmer
would stand in the shade, staring across his paddocks, rolling
more, slower cigarettes.

The boy was not surprised when he held his grandmother as
they watched the coffin lowered into the hole. 'Oh Stan,' she
whispered to her grandson's collar, 'Stan, Stan, Stan.' Just a
whisper of frail breath.

The cart was sold, and one of the horses went with it. The
other went to the knackery and shrieked in terror to be
separated from the mate it had pulled with all of its life.
Grandma Palmer covered her ears. 'Oh, Stan, Stan, what shall
we do?'

He watched the neighbour drive the cart away and looked down at the waterbag he'd retrieved from the axle. He pulled out the cork and drank the last drops from the neck of the bag and leant against the fence. He looked along the wires. How straight they were. He knocked at the post with the heel of his hand. How solid it was.

When he went back to the house, his grandmother was pulling a tray of pumpkin scones from the oven.

'Well, what do you expect, Alf?' she said, buttering scones with hectic slashes of the knife. 'There's no point crying over –' but she fell against his shoulder, the buttery knife all over his jacket.

'Oh Stan, Stan, Stan –' and the boy who had lost his Grandpa tried to stand there like one of the old man's posts. Tried to lash his quivering heart with bonds of fencing wire so that the old woman could lean there, tried to plant his feet like the horses when they set their shoulders into the traces, tried to replace the man who had gone.

She straightened and pushed him away at the length of her tiny arms, not bothering to wipe the wetness from her face.

'He loved you, Alf, and you deserved his love. Remember that.' The boy's heart strained its lashing of strung wire, but his teeth were set, his shoulders were squared, and his feet were rooted to the ground.

# THE CARBIDE LAMP

*I* was a boy. Say four or five. Sitting on a box in a disused fowl shed. Old crackling harnesses hung on hooks, webs billowed in the corners, powdered with dust. My shoulders were veiled in spiders' shawls as I took the carbide lamp and fingered the hemisphere of red glass, then the convex green. Fingering each in turn and looking deep into the colours of a richness never before equalled. The lamp had levers and chambers and handles and brackets, but I could not make it work.

Then my Papa was there, standing tall, looking at me through the wire netting, seeing a dusty boy following the coloured curves of glass with a finger. My eyes must have said, I can't make it go, because he took both me and the lamp against him and, then, beneath the passionfruit vine in deep shade and hanging ferns, his thick fingers would do magic over and around the lamp. Maybe it was the dimness, maybe his big hands, or maybe my looking at the big bones of his face, but I never followed the movements, and then we'd both be sitting watching the red and green lights flickering, glowing, and then beaming richer. Jewels. Ruby and emerald jewels, shone from that lamp. It was like we had the hugest gems of a richness few have looked upon.

And then Papa was dying. I watched him all in white, such a big man, white gowned, dwarfing all the others. He looked at me long and hard, and I walked away to look at the barley sugar shining golden in a jar. The jar was almost square with smooth corners and edges, and the gold in it shone out weakly onto a kidney dish, a faint glimmer. My Papa won't come out of here. They were all standing round him in clothes saying things. Some uncles had smiles on half their faces, and shifted from foot to foot, took up magazines and let them drop, turned to watch other visitors, said more things about cars, still with a smile on half their face, a quirk, and the aunties holding bags, making arrangements, practising for a death.

It was still there. I felt the round ruby, looked deep into the emerald. I turned the latches, I peered into the chambers, but I could not make it go. So I sat on the box hung around with cracking saddlery and forgotten webs and ancient chook manure and things that were familiar to me poked into the curves of corrugated-iron: a screwdriver, pliers, a piece of paper with writing on it, nails on a ledge, a bolt and a kerosene pump with a glass marble in it, green marble, bottle green. If you looked through the tin pipe to the sun, the sky was green like being in the sea. I could feel my hair floating about me like weeds. From my box I could sit and feel all of these things with my eyes, and later stand and handle each in turn. Next time my prints would be gone, but each thing was still there covered in dust as if it had never been moved. I thought of them, but most of all the ruby and emerald would glow on my wall at night.

The aunts and uncles said that Papa drank too much. Alcoholic was the word they said. And we, our family, went to church and hated beer and cigarettes, and we hurried past the doors of hotels. Bad men were in there, a gabble of drunkenness and the fume of sin, but I couldn't help looking down the iron gratings and seeing the barrels. We hurried past, and over our peas and potatoes and corn beef on Sundays, my Papa's drinking was discussed. He didn't earn enough money and he made his wife work and several times he disappeared. Where? They said a town, but I could never imagine him in a different hotel or anywhere else except under passionfruit and fern baskets. I always remembered him looking through chicken wire, his hand on my head and his big chest and the woollen hat. He went away, but where would he go? When they laid him in bed in white it was obvious he couldn't go anywhere. He was hemmed in by handbags and watches and shiny shoes, and he looked at me hard and long. The handbags and watches were talking over the huge block of the white clad man and didn't notice that I had to turn away and look into the amber of another dying man's barley sugar. The other man was in a dressing gown of red and green checks, listening to the radio at the other end of the ward, and so I could stare into the gold of his barley sugar and hope my Papa's eyes had not swivelled to follow me there.

One day, when I remembered, I went to the shed, and there was nothing. They dressed me, as they said, like a young man, and I wasn't to get dusty, but there was nothing in the shed, and so I went and asked them about the lamp and they couldn't remember it, although I said about the colours, but they couldn't remember a lamp like that and began to smile, at least on the half I could see of their face.

I've never liked hospitals and always try to get out. I always go late and read and drop magazines and sneak looks at my watch and wait to get out. Sometimes there are barley sugar bottles to look at, but not often, and I am tall with a tie and a watch and shifting feet and half a smiling face, and barley sugar has gone from the world and no one knows about carbide lamps.

# FRIDAY NIGHT

'Ay?' I looked up.

'Thank your mother for the rabbits.' It was the dopey kid from the next farm. He had a lisp that blurred the th's and furred the rabbits.

He was holding out a billy half full of milk, and I stopped mucking out the shed, looked over at our milkers ambling up the lane and then over my shoulder at the kitchen window where you could see my mother giving the pie dough Larry Dooley. The kid didn't take the hint.

I took the billy, and he vanished. Some people walk away and you can watch their backs until they go below the brow of the hill. This kid took two steps from you in an open paddock and just seemed to evaporate. I looked into the billy and could see a rim of cream three inches above the milk. He'd drunk half of it before he got to our place.

My mother heard the fly-wire door slam and turned as I put the billy on the table, her cheeks puffed like a fresh scone.

'Thank your mother for the rabbits,' I said, but as I turned to go out to the cows standing around scissoring their jaws, I could hear her calling after me. 'When you come in, Jack, there'll be meat on *your* plate, remember that.' I could

77

imagine her looking at the tide line in the billy and shaking
her head, clucky as a mother hen. She made us take rabbits
over to the Fergusons' farm, and they'd pay with what they
could, usually milk; like taking coals to Newcastle.

By the time I'd finished the cows, and they were waddling
back to the night paddock, I'd washed up and raced through
cleaning the cups and the milking gear. I missed the others.
Missed my brother. That kid was so smart. Draw and write!
You've never seen anything like it. Straight to uni down in the
smoke. First one of our mob educated ever.

Arthur could do anything. I never got jealous. As soon as he
was fourteen, fifteen, he could make me look like a cart-horse
when we played footy. He ran and dodged like a dancer. I'd be
grabbing the air where he'd been. When he played his first
game with our seniors, I knew he'd play league in Melbourne.
I went up for a mark and got flattened by a Golden Square
bloke; Arthur came from nowhere, split the bloke right up the
middle, grabbed the ball out of his hands and took off. He beat
'em all. I suppose as we clapped that goal we knew they'd
come up from town and snap him up. Afterwards in the rooms,
the old timers were already comparing him to Jesaulenko and
Bunton but all he said to me was, 'I got that bastard for yer,
mate.'

We'd go fishing down the river and build a little fire out of
cow pats to keep the mossies off, and we'd pull in a few redfin,
open a few cans and he'd start to sing. He'd do all the old bush
ones for me and then he'd sing in Latin. Church music. None
of us went for church much, but he must've picked it up in the
city. I tell you, the bush would shut up when Arthur sang. The
redfin'd get on the line just to hear him better.

Stupid aunties'd ask me and Aileen, 'Don't you mind about
Arthur, being so *brilliant?*' We didn't mind; it never occurred
to us to mind. We loved him I tell ya. Loved him like I was
never able to do again. My brother. Arthur was not like the rest
of people. There was something else about him. Blokes in the
footy club would stop telling dirty jokes when he came in the

shed, they'd clap him on the back and be mates, drink cans with him, and everything, but they knew he was different. None of us minded. He was ours.

We were so close all of us Palmers. Not just because of us having Arthur, but the whole thing. We all wanted to be with each other.

When we sat around the table the yarns'd start. Dad'd start the ball rolling with his impersonations of Murphy. Murphy and Dad shared a baler. They were good mates, I suppose, but Dad must have had to bite his tongue all the time because Murphy was such a silly coot.

I was hosing the cowshit out of the herringbones and giggling to myself as I imagined Dad letting his tongue loose after a week of baling with Murphy. Dad could take off anyone to a tee. He was the star turn at any country do for his jokes and imitations. The year we won the Grand Final, Dad turned on a barrel and kept everyone in tears doing imitations of every shopkeeper in the main street. No one took offence. If anyone else did that, it'd be bloody Winchesters at five yards.

Even the dog was allowed in on Friday night. Arthur home, Aileen knocked off work, the dog carrying on like a lunatic, and Dad ripping the tops off bottles of beer and winking at me as if to say, not bad, eh, Friday night. And poor old Mum, how she got tea on the table I'll never know.

Arthur would be telling us his latest batch of Melbourne jokes. Aileen would be carrying on like a married magpie, Dad revving up to bend our ears, and there's old Mum stoking the fire to make the pork crackle and trying to stop Dad from letting the dog drink the cat's milk. Like a bull in a crockery shop.

When we sat down to tea, Mum passed us our plates, and as she handed me mine I said, 'Thank your mother for the rabbits,' and I caught Dad with a mouthful of beer and he sprayed it all over Aileen. She screamed, the cat jumped out of its skin, and the dog took after it and brought down the pot plant, and the fern ended up in Arthur's roast.

'That's Grandma's fern!' yelled Mum.

'It's my bloody roast,' yelled Arthur. We were all howling with laughter, tears pouring down our cheeks.

Mum straightened up and wiped her eyes and went to get the gravy, and as she dished it up she said to me, 'All very fine to laugh at him, Jack, but as I said, there's meat on our table and, thank the Lord, laughter in our house.' That was supposed to make us feel chaste and Christian, and I suppose we all knew she was right, but it couldn't stop us from getting on with Friday night. We were subdued for a while and then Dad started on Murphy. He wrinkled up his face, and made his eyes bulge.

' "Have yer been seein' the balin' twine there, Stan, at all?"

' "Ar, no, Murph, but I seen that dog eatin' somethin'." Murphy turned around to his dog – bloody idiot Collie called Spud – and said to it, "And what would yer be doin' that for, now, Spud?" "P'raps he thinks it was time he was tied up," I sez, and Murph an' the dog looked 'round at me. I tell ya, it's tough work out at Murphy's, harder than you'd think, Mum. You reckon I'm having cucumber sandwiches out on the lawn. Not at all, at all. I've gotta educate Murphy and his dog and bale all the bloody hay from here to bloody Burrumbeet!'

With all the racket and the animals careering 'round I'm blowed if I know how we've got any of Mum's wedding crockery left!

I suppose that night out of all the mad Friday nights got stuck in my mind because a few weeks after Arthur got his marble pulled out of a barrel and was off to Vietnam. Tell you the truth, it was the first time we'd ever heard of the bloody place and all of a sudden we were waving him off on a plane headed for war.

'Where the bloody hell's Vietnam?' Dad screamed at the bloke in the army office.

'Asia, sir,' said the smart little prick from the public service. 'The prime minister has sent our troops there, to maintain the freedom of the people.'

'Well, why doesn't he send his own bloody sons, and some of his fuckin' Corgis too!' I was pretty sure Menzies didn't have Corgis, but that thought was swept from my mind as I caught Dad's eye. Saw him crying. Dad crying! I'd seen him get his hand caught in the maize machine and lose two fingers and a thumb, and all he did when I stopped the machine was hold up his hand and say, 'That'll stop me playin' marbles for a while.'

And here he was crying. 'I've bloody fought for this country once already, you bloody little twerp. How many fuckin' times have we got to do it?' It didn't make much difference, they sent Arthur anyway.

They killed him near as soon as he got off the plane. How could they? Arthur was so quick, such a bloody good shot. The little bastard was good at everything. I flew up to Sydney and saw his mate who'd been flown home without any eyes and no left arm.

'Pies,' said his mate, looking over my shoulder, 'bloody pies, mate. We were buying some pies off this weedy little slant kid, and she just blew up. They'd sent her out strapped with grenades. Arthur said, "That kid's bloody near starvin'," and dragged me over to buy her pies. Fuckin' pies.'

He had no eyes left, but there were still tears there. I didn't tell Dad. I didn't tell anyone. The Salvos picked me up and sent me home. Don't know how long I'd been wandering around pissed as an owl. Screaming and shouting in the street I was, rousing at poor bloody women, yelling at blokes that had nothing to do with it.

Anyway, I got home and I couldn't have timed it worse. I didn't know what day it was, literally, but when I looked up the calendar I saw it was a Friday, and I would have died, but Aileen came into the bathroom while I was still bawling my eyes out.

'Come on, Jack,' she said, 'don't squib it now. Mum and Dad

are waiting to know the worst.' So we got it over with, and Mum served up the Friday tucker, and Dad poured a beer and winked at me to cheer it up a bit. Someone had even taken the extra chair out to the verandah and put a pot plant on it, but it was never the same.

We got on with it, but it was never the same. Before then I'd never been conscious of time. Now I noticed things like Murphy's Collie dying, and even a small thing like that was like knocking a brick off my chimney.

When Aileen married the bloke from next door with the lisp, no one laughed. I half expected Dad to make a crack during the wedding speech about the rabbits, but he didn't. He started to say, 'I just wish –' and then he stopped and sat down suddenly. No one said boo until someone got the band playing the bridal waltz. Aileen, strong as a bloody north wind, had everyone up dancing and trying to make the best of it.

People around here will tell you that us Palmer men don't bother to shave, we just hammer the whiskers back in. We're supposed to be tough. But we're Sunday School teachers compared to the Palmer women. I've never seen Mum or Aileen give in. They set their teeth like bulldogs until whatever needed to be done was done. Then Aileen goes and marries the weedy bloke from the broken-down farm. I couldn't believe it. He was such a wet kid and here was Aileen in love with him! 'You can't,' I said to her, 'he's a bloody no hoper!'

'He can't play football, if that's what you mean,' she said, 'and he had bad luck with his parents, but he's come out of it a man, Jack, lisp or no lisp.'

After Dad died, Mum's arthritis got so bad she went to live with Aileen, while I wandered 'round playing for a different bush team each year. The pay was all right while it was winter, but my knees gave in eventually, so I came back to Burrumbeet and carted hay for Aileen's husband. It made me feel old and wasted, working someone else's farm.

Friday night. We sat in the kitchen after carting all day, and Mum was passing plates of roast around. Andrew, Aileen's husband, handed me my plate and I looked up into his eyes as he opened his mouth to speak. I remembered how we'd mocked him, and I imagined that he'd say, 'Thank your mother for the rabbits.' But he didn't, wasn't going to anyway. When he looked at me, he stopped whatever it was he was going to say, and just, said, 'Here you are, mate.' No lisp, no lisp at all. I started to laugh, laugh too much.

This year Andrew and I got about thirty bales to the acre off the two farms, and we had what Mum calls the harvest dinner. There was beer and wine and Aileen's kids drinking red cordial while they sat on my knee – but it's not the same.

Mum keeps her eye on me all the time, and everyone's careful what they say, too careful. I want someone to sing for me, someone to slap my back, make me laugh until the tears keep rolling down my face.

I suppose I wanted it to be Friday night forever.

# PRIMARY COLOURS

*Y*ou never expect it. It's like being eaten by a shark. It does happen, and people shed their redness on the waves, but it will never be from your waist that the shark snaps a morsel of kidney fat.

So here's Jackson, digging a row of fence post holes a mile long. The notch on the spade handle tells him when to stop digging. The string line and divot tell him where to start. Pleasantly hard work. Unpleasant oceans of mind-free time.

He looks out over the waving spring grass of the paddock and admires the lush growth of rye, clovers, paspalum and fescue. He helped the earth yield this fine pasture, and in the middle of the paddock are the follies. The grove of banksias he couldn't cut down. The tuft of scrub around the wombat-hole and several thickets for the resting place of travelling birds. And everywhere, single, fine, clean trunks of white gums, right down to the forest by the creek. Jackson's Folly. The hardest paddock to plough in East Gippsland, but the only one with resident kingfishers, eagles, emus, nightjars, bandicoots, snipe and ducks.

His heart took in the flight of the cuckoo-shrike, the sweep of the swallows and the tracks of kangaroos, snake and dingo.

This is his heart's place and here at his feet is his heart's blood.

His daughter. The grass is up to his knees. He can see her red hair hidden in the dark-green clover, and the kelpie's tail waves above the grass uncertainly. They are stalking each other. Suddenly they leap out, and she shrieks. The dog carouses, with short barks, and they tumble and roll in the long grass, delighting in a long deliberate roll to the bottom of the hill. They're both mad, both mates.

They play like this every day while Jackson slams the crowbar into clay. Each morning when they arrive, the dog courses the playing field, checking for black snakes. There are none anymore, their smells have staked out the place.

His back has had it. He can split a hundred posts a day and dig sixty holes. Feel like an Anzac. Fall the tree, billet the log, bark the billets, split the posts, dig the holes, tamp the post, run the wire, hang the gate on corner posts the tractor can't lift. And now? All for nothing. It's over. The selection, the vow – down the drain. Mistakes.

The shadow of his favourite white gum tells him it's half an hour past lunch, and he calls to the two ginger pelts. The dog leaps through the grass with her back curved like a whippet, the tongue everywhere, the eyes ecstatic. The girl comes tumbling after, shouting, screaming with joy, the hair a nest of lovely copper, the arms flinging with the delicious energy of young animals.

Jackson's mood is set by the plunge of the bar, the gouge of the spade, the lift and tip of earth, and the wound of thoughts. This metronome is invaded by the two rampant beasts who tumble and screech, upsetting sandwiches and themselves.

She loves this. She doles out the sandwiches and drinks. Jackson gets his own coffee because she can't lift the steel thermos, but she pours her cordial and hands out the dog's biscuits, which the kelpie eats like a 'good dog', enjoying the ceremony as much as the girl.

Jackson sits with his back to the old white gum, girl and dog

85

draped across his knees. The remnants of lunch in disorder around them.

Jackson watches the movement in the grass as wood ducks waddle down to the creek, and he sees Van Gogh's waving grasses, the wind making patterns on the nap of green plush while the kingfisher sings at the nest. God is surely in His heaven, but this man struggles to cap off his tear ducts.

'Rain, Dad, it's gunna rain.' Dog and daughter are up searching the perfect blue sky. He mumbles about the ducks shaking water off their feathers as they fly by, but it doesn't matter, lunch is over, the frolic has begun.

There are the beautiful primary colours. Absolute azure in the sky, rich green of the grass and the red of dog's tail and child's hair. His heart surges with the beauty.

The crowbar wavers, the spade stops shovelling. Jackson packs up the tools and calls to the gambollers in the grass. They collect a few stones, call out down the wombat burrow a few times, look for four-leaf clovers, collect petrified wood from up by the tractor and play in the grass. A formula for daily bliss.

They bound after him through the grass. Down at Duck Hole the blackies quack and ogle and paddle off to the further end. Father and daughter strip off, watched by the dog who isn't so keen on the swimming bit.

Daughter sits on the little jetty while Jackson swims a slow length in the icy water. He glides with his head just above the surface, and the ducks allow him to come among them, ogling with stupid alarm. Goodness, goodness, look at that!

The girl has the big tractor tube ready when he swims back, and together they paddle about the pond while the kelpie is frantic on the bank and tries to eat water and gum trees.

Apricot glows above the trees, and more ducks and cormorants fly in while they dress.

Walking up the hill, the evening settles like the murmur of a woman's voice, and Yellow Robins sing the end of the day. The Lyre Bird clicks in the scrub as they plod on to home.

Home.

Smoke straggles away from the chimney, the generator chugs, they can even smell things cooking. Daughter dashes in, tugging stones and cicada shells out of her pockets as she goes.

The kelpie and Jackson bring in the cow to the little bark-roofed bail. The jersey chomps away at the oats, and rolls her huge dark eyes.

Those eyes with their long lover's lashes. Jackson presses his face into her side and the cow takes a step to spread her weight.

Milk drills into the tin bucket and in the rhythm of this lovely flesh-flesh movement, both are content. Ease for her, milk for him. He breathes in her lovely cow smell and watches the sky flooding with vermilion behind the trees. The Yellow Robin is piping its last message, the cormorant plops into the dam, and the world closes its day with such careless grandeur. Ten million such symphonies, and each time such sad, beautiful, perfect joy.

Jackson stands with the bucket and releases the jersey. She presses her oaty muzzle against his leg as she ambles off to her calf. The man looks up to the house on the hill, lights aglow in the window, smoke a mauve smudge from the chimney and a full bucket of milk. What could be more perfect?

Perfect.

# FUNNY MAN

*E*verybody who bothered to look noticed that he was a short man with a stomach already hanging like a pudding in his shirt and breasts becoming pendulous. But you didn't notice until he looked up at you that his eyes crossed inwards that neither eye looked straight at yours.

He lifted his case from the station platform and stood for a moment staring at the sign that said 'Shepparton'. Another country town. If anybody had looked twice, what was it they would have noticed? A hesitancy, an air of sustained dread? He turned from the station sign and looked for the car that might be waiting for him.

He walked the length of the platform and turned in through the green wicket gate, and a man was there waiting – predictably large.

'You must be Bobby McLean,' said the man and lifted a huge knotted hand. Bobby looked at the hand, realizing that he must shake it. He put his suitcase down and let his hand be gripped by this beaming giant. 'Yes, that's right, Bobby McLean,' and the Scots accent was more or less proof of his credentials. Bobby could see that the man looking down at him had noticed his crossed eyes and was wondering if there had been a mistake at the agency, but Bobby lifted his case and prepared to follow.

'Here, give us that mate. I'm Jack Shearer, president of the Shepp footy club. I rang you up last week.' Yes, Bobby remembered the voice. Jack took hold of the case and concentrated his gaze on their destination, the Railway Hotel.

'Jesus, this could all be a bugger of a mistake,' Jack thought as he marched down the ramp past the pepper trees.

'Well, there you are,' said Jack, 'the Railway Hotel, not flash but comfortable enough. We'll leave your case in the lobby and go in and see some of the boys in the bar.'

A few looked up with greetings and jokes for Jack and then dropped their eyes to the short man beside him. There seemed to be an almost imperceptible lull in the conversation, and Jack said, 'Well fellas, here's Bobby McLean, the comedian we got from Melbourne for the ball tonight.'

Eyes lifted up from glasses, faces were extracted from conversations, and all turned to look at the man who was said to be a comedian of huge repute – or so the agency had billed him – Bobby McLean, sensational cabaret artist!

Now was the time for a joke, Bobby thought, get 'em quick, prove yourself; but he was too tired, he had stood like this, next to huge, ageing ruckmen too many times, watched too often by too many expectant faces. So he said, instead, 'I hear you've got good cold beer up here. I'd better sample some, I suppose.' That would have to do. Praising their beer, although it never won instant rapport, at least never offended anyone.

The men at the bar were undecided whether the Scottish accent was a sign of promise, but they were encouraged by the easy disappearance of the beer down the comedian's throat.

Jack remembered himself and asked after Bobby's journey.

'How'd the old rattler treat ya, Bobby?'

'Good, quite comfortable,' said Bobby, and began drinking the beer that Jack had bought him. A conversation began around him about sheep and fruit and then got around to football – a post mortem of the Grand Final that Shepparton had won three weeks ago. How many times had each mark, handball and shirtfront been discussed in those three weeks, Bobby wondered, as he slid more liquid down his throat, happy to have his face hidden behind a pot of beer. They began talking about the Best and Fairest presentations that were to be made at tonight's ball, and inevitably one of the group turned and said,

'Gunna tell a few jokes tonight, are ya, Billy? Hope they'll be clean,' and winked and laughed, huh, huh, huh. Bobby decided not to correct him about his name, but Jack swallowed, wiped his mouth and said, 'His name's Bobby McLean, and it doesn't matter what the jokes are like, everyone's broadminded here.'

'What about giving us a sample then, Bi – Bob,' said the man who seemed to end every question with three quick indecisive laughs. Bobby had the glass to his lips, and nobody saw that his eyes were closed. In that short second behind the beer glass, he gained some comfort, but he couldn't prevent his mind from wondering if the man had ever asked anyone a question without following it up with a triple half-hearted laugh.

When he opened his eyes and put down his glass, the group were watching him, and it was clear that he could not escape telling a joke. They had all noticed his crossed eyes by now and were beginning to have their doubts, and Jack who had hired a comedian instead of a stripper began worrying about how to explain an investment of a hundred and fifty dollars. The rest of the footy club committee had ideas about a stripper turning it on for the boys and got quite nasty when Jack decided against Simone the Sequined Siren. If Jack made up his mind, however, there weren't many who voted against him – not enough, anyway.

'I suppose,' began Bobby, taking a deep breath, the shudder of which only he felt, 'I suppose you've all heard about the Irish dog that got caught in a rabbit trap. Chewed off three legs and was still caught.' The gusts of laughter came hesitantly, and Jack took a breath. 'What about the man in hospital who woke up in the morning and called out, 'Nurse, nurse, I can't feel my legs!' 'Of course you can't,' said the nurse, 'the doctor cut off both your arms last night!' They really enjoyed that. Bobby took a drink and wondered if he could tell one more joke and then pretend to go to the toilet. He was sweating and could smell himself.

'Did you hear about the two men standing at the bar, and one of them had a dog beside him. The first man said, "Does your dog bite?" The other man said, "No, my dog doesn't bite." So the first man bent down to pat the dog on the head, and the dog went gna, gna, and chewed his hand. "I thought you said your dog doesn't bite," the first man said, and the other said, "I didn't say that was my dog." ' They slapped Bobby on the shoulder and someone bought him a beer. Amputee jokes never failed to get a laugh, thought Bobby as he swallowed his beer and excused himself to go to the toilet.

He urinated against the stainless steel and noticed the brand on the urinal, Mira. There were a lot of Miras. Coscos were pretty common too, and occasionally you saw a Sunrise or a Caroma. Mira, Mira on the wall, he thought as he shook off the droplets and zipped himself up.

Jack came in as he began to wash his hands in the grubby porcelain basin.

'Ah, there you are, thought we'd lost ya for a minute. Now look, if there's anything you need, just let me know.' Jack faced the stainless steel and spoke over his shoulder. 'Harry's taken ya bag up to ya room, counter teas start in a few minutes and the ball starts at eight in the GV room. Come over a bit before then and I'll show ya the lie of the land.' Jack zipped himself up and looked down at Bobby as he stood beside him at the basin. Jack was still not convinced that this little man could hold an audience of footballers flushed from beer and checking out the women.

'Another beer, Bob?' Jack asked without much enthusiasm.

'No thanks,' said Bobby. 'I'll go up to my room and clean up a bit before tea.'

In his room, he gazed out of the first-floor window across the corrugated-iron verandah roof to the other side of Main Street. A black and white dog was sniffing along the street outside all the closed shops, licking up something outside the milk bar – probably some bawling kid's ice cream, thought Bobby, and turned back to the musty bed to unpack his case and find his toilet bag. He stopped in the centre of the room clutching the bag to his chest and hung his head. If anyone had been looking, they would have noticed him stand there for some minutes, and anyone close enough would have seen how tightly his eyes were clenched. But there was no one close enough, and no one looking.

He walked down the thready carpet of the corridor which every bush hotel has, past all the anonymous doors and found the bathroom, which looked down over the railway yards and pepper trees. Two boys played with the switch gear. There was a black and white dog there too, but it was probably a different one.

The water was hot. It wasn't always, and he let it play over the back of his neck and over his hair and across his shoulders. No one else did the country town footy dos; all the other gag men stuck to the pubs and, better still, the RSL clubs.

The bush was hard work for a city slicker and the pay was crook and they expected the show to last most of the weekend. They either slapped your back a lot and tried to be as funny as they thought you were, or they were like Jack, slightly disappointed. Most people expect to get Ronnie Barker or Dave Allen. Ah well, the water was hot and his muscles responded to it drumming on his back.

He ran his hand through the hair that grew on his chest and across his shoulders. He had big shoulders. Sure, he had a pot, but he couldn't help wearing his shirt unbuttoned enough to show his chest and his gold medallion hidden in the black curls. Sure, it looked a bit sleazy, but that chest was all he had going for him; his eyes were a distinct disadvantage. They were what had led him into telling jokes – everybody seemed to expect it of him – a man with crossed eyes.

He ate his gravy-soaked roast in the lounge. The triangle of bread and butter would no doubt be stained brown with gravy underneath. He lifted it to see, and there was the spongy messy pulp. If I was a cook, I'd never do that, he thought and swallowed clots of beef and sprouts, but pushed the bread aside.

Jack met him in the GV room. What the hell did GV stand for? thought Bobby as Jack showed him to the small stage in front of the tables laid out in the club colours. He tapped at the mike, which looked decidedly unreliable and which he knew no one would remember to lower from ruckman height.

Some of them wore burgundy dinner suits, most wore outdated lounge suits, and some didn't bother. The women mostly wore long frocks. Some well trussed in psychedelic caftans, some nubile in gowns that slipped like silver along their curves, but the rest were country girls tending to awkwardness inside formal dresses of cheap pastel shades.

Bobby was seated at the table of officials, all ex-footballers who had gone to fat or baldness and whose sponge-cake wives dished out pies every Saturday. All the perms and lashings of after-shave were fairly convincing early on; but soon the first wisps of hair began to betray the coiffures and the first hairy armpits to exude the Old Spice. During the presentation of awards there were a lot of local jokes called across the hall, and the men around Bobby began to tell slightly risque yarns and kept glancing at Bobby, inviting him to tell a stunner.

The paper tablecloths became soggier, the hairdos began to disintegrate, shirt sleeves were rolled up and by the time Bobby caught Jack's signal to go back-stage, the whole room was in a state of uproar, cigarette smoke, burst balloons and beer-soaked crêpe streamers.

At last Jack took the microphone and, trying to impress on the audience that they were about to be dazzled by a city comedian, introduced Bobby McLean. By the way he kept glancing to the side, you could see that Jack was unsure whether this little man could grab any more attention from this ribald crowd than he had done.

Bobby let them yell and catcall and deliberately lowered the microphone to his own height, then stood looking over the audience. He had done this a hundred times and was undismayed by the riot before him.

At last he leant close to the microphone and called out to the most riotous and dishevelled larrikin drunk, 'Hey, come over here, come on out, let's have a look at you!' The drunk was reluctant. He was happiest standing among a mob and flicking beer mats at anyone in front of him. 'Come on son, don't be shy, you're a big boy now, come out and let's have a look at you.' The youth, urged by his mates, was caught between cowardice and courage and ambled to the microphone.

'Now, take a look at this, folks. Have you ever seen anything quite as sharp as this?' The crowd roared 'No-ooooo!' 'Come on son, tell us your secret. Who's your tailor?' The crowd roared again, and the youth gladly fell back among the crowd. Bobby knew that he nearly had them and launched into his first amputee joke, but kept his eye and ear on the mood of the mob. Another local lad tried his luck at being the town comic-gladiator and yelled out, 'Ah, get out mate, we heard that one at state school.' Bobby almost gasped with relief and leant into the mike, perfectly pitching his voice at the audience – the advantage of amplification.

'We're in luck here, folks, because next year we're getting Evel Knievel up, and he's going to try and jump this bloke's mouth!' The crowd roared as Bobby told his salvo of Irish, mother-in-law and wife jokes.

'Now, ladies, I hope you won't be offended if I mention a subject that people are usually afraid to discuss in public.' A woman, excited by laughter, alcohol and no kids around, shouted, 'Ar, come off it, sport, you can't embarrass me, I do it all the time.' 'Well, there you are, folks,' said Bobby, walking over to the woman and pointing at her, 'here's a woman who farts all the time.' The crowd laughed and roared again at the skill of this man parrying every abuse, thrusting with derision and humiliation. He then began a series of jokes that concentrated on farting and shitting. His audience wept with laughter, but Bobby's face was expressionless except when he made a farting or shitting noise into the microphone. They loved every blurting ppppppppppffffffff. After Bobby's last joke he left immediately and the crowd clapped and cheered.

Bobby mopped his brow. 'Did 'em again,' he said as he stood at the back door, taking a deep breath of the night air that smelled of pepper trees and dust. He joined the ball as they danced to the local 50-50 band. Where else could you still see people doing the twist? He accepted the first free beer pushed into his hands as he sat at a table with a couple of other men. One was telling him that he had a joke that Bobby would really enjoy. Bobby closed his eyes for only a fraction of a second and a barely discernible shudder quivered across his shoulders, but his glass was up to his lips and nobody noticed.

He endured the joke he had heard and told before and sat without flinching while another man demanded to hear a truckie joke. Bobby told a truckie joke, and a small group developed. The young man he had embarrassed about his clothing stabbed a finger at him and said, 'I suppose you reckon you know a joke about everything, do you?' 'Yes,' said Bob, 'you name a subject, and I'll tell you a joke about it.' The young man wasn't ready for this and said, 'All right, all right, well tell me a joke about – about – about a horse.' So Bobby instantly began a joke about a horse, and the youngster fell back once again among the crowd.

He was everyone's favourite now, and beers kept appearing in his hands. He was invited to a party after the ball, and as the band began to pack away their drums and guitars Bobby was herded into the lobby while his companions lugged out car fridges full of melted ice and the rest of the cans.

The party was in a weatherboard house surrounded by dusty clots of garden and rusty shells of cars. Inside all the lights

were glaring off slopped linoleum and laminex. Music blared
out country rock, and Bobby glanced with an expert's eye at
the gold toast-rack record stand and noticed enough Slim
Dusty and truckie records to break his heart.

He wandered out to the yard to the clear night air of stars
and the persistent perfume of peppercorns. A curlew called in
the swamp behind the rail yards and a young footballer
coughed and vomited behind the chook shed. Bobby urinated
in a patch of straggly geraniums, and the young footballer
lurched inside to drink more cans. The Best and Fairest.

A woman came out of the lino lavatory still brushing down
her skirt or perhaps she was drying her hands. She gently
collided with the doorjamb, laid a restraining hand on the
funny man's shoulders, and looked into his eyes. Were they
crossed or were hers? 'Bobby, isn't it, Bobby?' He nodded. She
put an arm around his shoulder, and he could feel her breast
pressed against him as she pulled him towards the lounge-
room. 'Come here, Bobby, and I'll show you something really
funny. You're a comedian, you'll like this.' She pointed to a
corner of the room where a man was slumped on the carpet in
foetal position, his arms folded and a crêpe paper party hat on
his head.

'See that, Bobby, that's the six foot ruckman I married, the
bronzed bulldozer driver. That's what you end up with,
Bobby.' She looked into his eyes again and began to feel sure
that it was his eyes that were crossed. She looked down at his
medallion and took it in her hand, her fingers straying through
the hair of his chest. Still looking at the medallion she said,
'Why so quiet, Bobby? You're the funny man, you're supposed
to be the life of the party.' She replaced the medallion on his
chest and stroked the curly black fur.

'G'day, Bob,' said Jack, and pushed a stubby at him. 'Debbie
chattin' ya up already, is she? She's a bloody devil, aren't ya,
Deb?' and he tried to pat her bum.

'Piss off, Jack,' she snapped and pushed her way out to the
kitchen. Jack's eyes followed her. 'Terrific tits on that woman,

mouth like a garbage bin, and morals to match. Anyway, Bobby boy, how are things?' said Jack, not much interested in the answer. The night had been a success, the crowd loved the comedian, and now he was drunk with relief and was soon gone.

Bobby saw Debbie coming back with a glass and ducked behind a few ruckmen and went outside to sit on a low brick fence with gaps like a decayed mouth. One of the cars parked in the street was rocking violently and Bobby lit a cigarette and looked out into the stars, and wondered how he could fill in the time until tomorrow's 2.35 pm train. An old black and white dog ambled arthritically towards him and slumped his backside against Bobby's feet and never looked at him once. Made no move to attract a pat from the man sitting on the fence – just something in the night to sit near. Bobby looked down at the matted fur on the head of the worn-out sheepdog and patted the muzzle and ears. The dog made no move. The two continued to sit together in the night as the car before them rocked and the sounds of a disintegrating party reached them from the house.

A hand was laid on Bobby's shoulder and he turned to see Debbie swaying in front of him. 'I've been looking for you, Bobby,' she said and nudged the dog out of the way with her foot. 'Thought you could get away from me, didn't you? Well, you're wrong, funny little Bobby boy, 'cause I've found you,' and she took his arm and led him along down the street between the sugar gums that rattled their bark and leaves in the night breeze. They stopped under some peppercorns, and as she drew his mouth to hers the musky odour of the peppercorn trees was replaced by the musk of a woman.

'You haven't asked where I'm taking you, have you?' Bobby didn't answer as he looked through the trellises of the weeping foliage.

'I'm taking you back to your hotel room, that's where I'm taking you,' and she ran her hands beneath his shirt. 'Cold, Bobby boy, I'd better put you to bed.'

Bobby's eyes were awake first. The dawn light was coming through the holland blinds in a brown-golden glow that threatened a broiling day. The breeze moved the blind. He could feel the nakedness of the woman beside him and could smell the rich, thick musk on his hands and on the sheets.

The woman groaned, and she turned and slung an arm across his chest. In this light there was a certain classical beauty about the tousle of her hair and the curve of breast and hip. The light gilded her cheek, and her eyes, closed in sleep, were like a child's sleeping fitfully over a threatening dream.

She groaned again and stirred, and her eyes flicked awake. She pushed a hand across her face and through her hair. Why did people do that when they woke up?

'Jesus,' said Debbie, as a recollection crept beneath the lids of her eyes and she recognized the hairy chest and crossed eyes of the funny man – her lover. 'Jesus! Back home to Prince Charming – this should be good for a couple of black eyes!'

Bobby went off to shower as she dressed quickly and gathered her bag and shoes ready for a dawn retreat to her weatherboard house and a hiding.

She came into the bathroom and spoke through the sound of spattering water and curling steam. 'Well, Bobby, I'm off into the dawn light!' She fidgeted with her bag and slipped her shoes on. Bobby was immersed in steamy water and dread.

'Aren't you going to speak to your lover?' and she looked at the shower curtain. 'The earth didn't exactly move, I know, but it never does, do you think? But that was nice, anyway –' She looked up from her bag and tore the shower curtain aside and stared at the back of the portly man with thinning hair. She kissed his back quickly and squeezed his shoulder. 'See you later, Bobby.' Her heels squeaked on the tiles as she walked away and he turned to watch as she left, struggling, urging himself to say something comforting, but his teeth were shut hard. The water drummed on his shoulders, streaming in rivulets through the hair on his chest.

He heard the whistle as he stood on the gravel platform and lugged his case towards the edge of the siding. The only passenger for the 2.35. Another hundred miles of dry country track and three lonely hours of clackety clack.

# THAT'S WHAT FRIENDS ARE FOR

We could hear the yip yip yip of Yellow-Bellied Gliders, and the boobook owl. Boo book, boo book. The billy hung across the fire, and the aromatic burning of the wattle mingled with the smoke from our cigarettes.

I turned to see if Steve was as conscious of the aesthetics as I was. The moon latticed by the eucalypts had cast diamonds of light across his face and chest so that he looked like one of the more sinister commedia characters. When he spoke, I could see only one eye and a fragment of his mouth. His disembodied hand holding the cigarette rested across his chest and gestured at the night with glowing ash.

'We used to do this all the time when we were kids. Remember?' I didn't answer, but murmured, made a noise with my mouth that always encouraged people to continue talking. I hated talking, but left people thinking I was a good conversationalist. Steve knew me too well for that, but continued anyway.

'The dogs and the owls used to scare the shit out of us, remember. We'd cower in our tents. Now we know too much. We know it's beautiful and think of music and paintings.

100

Chopin nocturnes. David Davies.'

The boobook called and the creek was talking to itself among the rocks. Creeks are gentle, domestic. Perhaps Davies was the right painter for tonight. But he usually painted twilights. I struggled to think of a night painting of the Australian bush, but apart from Streeton's bushfires I couldn't remember one.

'It's beautiful, isn't it?' He turned to me, the other eye lit by a diamond of moonlight, and the whole mouth was in umbra. Of course it was beautiful, but there was no lift in my heart. Not like when we were kids and would crest the ridge of a sand dune and look at the luminous white foam from breaking waves that snarled on the black sea. The heart became a chorus then. Beethoven if we'd known.

Now beauty was recognized, but the heart didn't leap. The spirit didn't rise like an escaped breath. We could describe it now, compare it with art, but not be writhen with the passion of it.

His eye still looked at me, and the end of the cigarette glowed suddenly crimson where the mouth must be.

'Yes, of course,' I said, to make the eye look away, resume its attention to the scraps of constellar patterns between the clumps of gum leaves. 'Of course, it's beautiful. Idyllic.' We lay on our backs, smoking in our idyll. The glider still yipped and a frog was gulping on the creek bank.

Steve rolled onto one elbow, flicked his butt into the fire and stared at the embers, a full profile in moonlight, the pallid face tinged with rose.

'What could be more perfect, do you think?' His eyes turned to me, glittering with the icy light of the moon. He knew how to talk to me.

'Mmm,' I said, sitting up and hugging my knees, 'there could be a –'

'Woman who loved you?' He finished my sentence, but I wasn't sure that's what I would have said. That's what I felt but not what I would have said. He knew me too well –

'Well – yes – a woman that you loved,' I said, my heart's tendons beginning to restrict my chest.

'And one you would love in return – equally.' His face, stellar-white, fixed mine with its bright eyes. I shrugged my shoulders.

'Did you know – with you it's hard to tell what you know – that she'd gone?' I stared into his face transfixed like the bandicoot by the owl. The owl's trick is to keep staring.

'Yes, she left. Who would have thought, eh? That she would get up and leave after all that has happened.'

I threw my cigarette into the fire. The action of fingers giving the eyes excuse for flight.

'Do you still love her?' he asked. I concentrated on the fire.

'Of course, you do. That's you, isn't it? True to the end. You're born out of your time. Really. Guinevere was the girl for you. Or Rapunzel. I bet you dream that you throw pebbles, white round pebbles, at her window, and she opens the casement – because it would have to be a casement – and she lets down her hair and you climb, climb, climb . . .

'She cut it off, you know. "You only love me for my hair," she said. And cut it off. Just like that. Snip, snip, snip, last man's head, head, off. Snip.' His fingers snipped a diamond out of the nets of moonlight.

He picked up his gun.

'Come on then, Lancelot, let's get those bunnies and get on with the boyhood lantern show.'

From the hill the rabbits could be seen easily as they bobbed like squat caterpillars from one patch of grass to the next. Their tails shone. An evolutionary mistake? Hard to tell. Following a running rabbit in the sights of a rifle the tail was a distraction, the eye aimed at the white bobbing tuft. But when they were still it was just sufficient to find your mark. Still, there were lots of them. Hard to tell about evolution. My mind playing hide and seek with my heart. So she cut off her hair, and she's left him. Where is she then?

The blast opened a chasm in the moonlight, and I turned to see a rabbit kick and flop. The others bounded away, then sat on haunches to sniff. I lifted my rifle. Crack! Another rabbit was flung into the air by the trauma of its muscles. The rest ran for cover, and Steve crept down to bring them back into the line of his sights. He turned and looked up at me to make sure that I'd seen him so that I wouldn't fire. He gave the old signal that we had used all those years ago to register the safety of firing lines. We both smiled at the boy scoutishness of it all. Like old times. So she'd cut off her hair –

He aimed at another rabbit, and it kicked and flopped. Her hair. I raised my gun and he stood up in front of me, signalling.

'Well, go on,' he called.

'What?'

'There's a hare.' Hair. He was scrambling up through the bracken. 'There's a hare near the rock, look.' He pointed, but the hare was already sprinting for the wattle by the creek. My barrel tracked and levelled. This wasn't fair. The hare leapt, plumped to the ground and kicked in a lazy circle.

'Well, you got it. I thought you'd lost your touch. Or did you just want a moving target?'

'I was waiting for you to have another shot. I wasn't really watching.' He cuffed my shoulder and gave a short laugh.


He watched as I pulled the fur over its shoulders and cut off its head.

Once, our dogs would have been sitting on the other side of the fire not missing a trick.

'You know, I don't think she's all that attractive without her hair. Perhaps she was her hair. To us. I wonder what the knight would have done if Rapunzel –. Your Mick must be dead now, surely.'

'Yeah, years ago. Dad and I are working one of his pups that we got out of Kelly.'

'Any good?'

'Probably the best yard dog we've had. Mitchell we called him.'

'Mitchell?'

'Out of the Lawson stories. You know, Mitchell says this, Mitchell says that. Dad reckoned that he speaks up as good as Mitchell. Good bark in the yard. What about your old heeler?'

'Blue?' said Steve, watching me spring the hare's skin on a green wattle fork. 'Oh, old Blue died years back. I was still on the farm. Picked up a bait. Had to shoot him. What are you going to do with the fur?' I hung it from a hakea shrub and looked at it.

'Dunno. Dad makes things out of them. Tans them with wattle bark and makes slippers and things. I always keep the skins, just a habit I suppose. Dad'll never make that many moccasins out of them.'

Two rabbits roasted above the coals, and we drank beer, listening to the mopoke and the frogs. The glider had gone. I sharpened a stick and pushed it into the haunch of a rabbit to see how they were going. Red juice crept out of the hole and spat into the fire. We stared into the flames, blue-green and gold where the rabbit's blood spattered the coals.

'What will you do now?' I asked, as I stared at the fire. Out of the corner of my eye I could see his face as he turned towards me. White marble shot by rosy flames.

'About her, you mean?'

'Mmm.'

'Well, nothing. She's gone – flown the coop. No great shock, old son. We'd been at each other's throats for years.'

'Do you know where she – well, where –'

'Where she's gone, you mean? Oh, I've got a few ideas, but it's not all that important. Nothing'll change. That's it.'

'Why'd you come back here? Did you think she'd be at her Mum's place?'

'No, I come to see you. Me old mate. Times of trouble. You know. A man's best friend is his friend.' His lips parted on the joke, and his teeth glistened with moisture. I turned the potatoes in the bed of coals.

Steve opened more cans while I served the rabbits. We cut the potato jackets and soaked their white flesh in melting butter.

'That's rosemary, isn't it?' Steve said, holding up a rabbit leg and testing the flavour in his mouth.

'And oregano.'

'Where'd you learn about cooking with herbs?' he said, staring at me over the bone as he bent his head to angle his teeth to the flesh.

'Oh, there were these old gypsies wandering through, and they taught me to cook and read palms, turn lead into gold, men into wolves –' He snorted with his mouth full of rabbit.

'Mum's got a yard full of herbs, and I have a jar full in the truck for when I go fishing. Nice on redfin. The twentieth century reached Tungamah a couple of years back. We even saw the America's Cup on television. In colour.'

His eyes laughed. 'I thought some local school teacher might have been introducing you to the finer arts.'

'No such luck. Our local school teacher smokes a pipe and belongs to Apex. Don't think he can boil water,' I said, wiping up meat juice with the potato. We stacked our plates and sat back with our arms on our knees, staring at the fire, prodding at half-burnt sticks with our boots. Only the small sounds of the night.

'I did think she was at her mother's – or your place.' His eyes were on my face again, knowing that I'd have to reply.

'No, mate,' I said, not looking up, 'and the telegraph hasn't reported any new arrivals at her Mum's.'

'Ah well, I'm blowed if I know then. I've looked everywhere. It's not surprising.' His voice had dropped a register, and my shoulders stiffened as I'd seen dogs do before they even knew they were afraid.

'I hit her, you see, kicked her.' I stared around at him. Kicked her. No! Kicked *her*!

105

'Not hard, but I guess it was enough. I was drunk, and we were screaming –'

'Drunk!' I said. 'Drunk, and you kicked her!' The boo book stopped. I'd shouted. 'Drunk!'

'Men do get drunk, old son.'

'And *kick* –' I stumbled to my feet and stared down at him. Enough time to collect myself. I walked a few steps from the fire and took in a lungful of cold night air. When I turned back I was calmer, and he had his eyes down. As I settled by the fire to pour the mugs of coffee, he looked towards my face. I could feel his eyes upon me, and I knew there was supplication in them. Kicked her – he kicked her. I passed him his coffee and the action of hand passing and hand reaching meant that our eyes had to meet, and he knew enough to hold mine.

'Listen,' he said, 'I'm not asking you to say, "There, there boy, it'll be all right, it wasn't your fault – " I didn't come to be forgiven. I came to ask you to look out for her, and to tell me if she turns up.' The boobook had started again. 'Please mate, if she turns up, give me a ring.'

I raised the coffee to my mouth and let my eyes escape behind the blue enamel rim.

'That's what friends are for, isn't it? Isn't that what they say?' The coffee was hot, and I put the mug on the ground, slopping it as the mug tilted on a twig and the shaking of my hand.

'Listen,' I said, swallowing between each sentence, 'if she comes back here, I'm not going to promise any bloody thing, Steve. I love her –'

'You loved Rapunzel. This is a forty-year-old woman we're talking about. My wife. Not your fair lady, not your maiden in distress.' Our voices had the cold steadiness of moonshine, the flat dull ring of pewter beaten by the stern hammers of our tongues.

We kicked the coals together while I threw the plates into a bucket and packed the food away from possums. We were adult. We were calm. The table had to be cleared, the house kept in order.

106

I could see his hunched shape trellised by moonlight as I made a pillow of my boots rolled in an old coat. I stretched out and stared at the great disc of the moon dodging among the leaves. And, as with every other night of my life, I thought of her. I chased the image of her, trying to catch a glimpse to see if her face was older or her hair still long. Rapunzel, Rapunzel, what was the image I brought into the heliograph each night? Was it a thumb-worn silicon slide or did I love her? Love her.

'There's an early dew, mate.' He must have turned over to watch me, seen the moonlight seek out the small crystal on my cheek. 'Just do us a favour and ring me. I'm not expecting her to – but I would like to know where she was.' His voice was quiet, so quiet that the wood smoke seemed to carry his words away.

My teeth had found the old grooves of their grinding, but as I breathed in air from the night the quivering in my chest was stilled by the chill of moonshine.

'Okay, I'll ring you,' my voice said, clumsy between my teeth and tongue, my jaw aching with its tightness.

'That's what mates are for,' he said, his voice under harness again. 'Isn't that what they say?'

# NEITHER DID I

*J*ohnny and me were mates. I was a kid, still a bit apple-pink in the cheeks, and Johnny was thirty-three, still entirely optimistic despite being sacked from more jobs than he'd had hot dinners.

We poured beers and mopped floors, cleaned up vomit and carried sleeping drunks out to the bus-stop bench. If there was a fight, Johnny would go out and get the boss and not come back, and I would get the Pacifier, a three foot iron bar that bolted the doors, and swing it in gentle revolutions around the room. The fight would usually stop, not out of fear, but because this was about the best show most of them had seen since Roy Rene put his fingers through his gloves.

Johnny would come back about this time, having failed to find the boss. Johnny and me were mates.

At lunchtime we would get our sandwiches from the German deli across the street, and when Gunther got the pension and a peaked cap with ear flaps (such are the rewards in life), a woman took over the shop.

The counter lunches at the Rawburn Hotel were avoided by staff who'd seen the kitchen and the tattooed arms of the day cook, and so Johnny came back with his sandwiches one day and gave me a sly wink.

'Divorcee,' he winked aloud, 'I can smell it over the counter. Tremendous tits, too.'

'She's got a little girl as well,' I said, still in the grip of Presbyterian Sunday School morals. Johnny didn't hear or care, he was eating his salad sandwich, beetroot staining his lips and sliced lettuce dangling from his chomping jaws.

We opened the bar doors to the black and grey shades of a Rawburn Street grimed by the dust and noise of the railway station. We hosed down the gutters, and last night's drunken dreams and retched memories went down the drain with the burst-eyed cat run down in the night.

At night we closed the doors on the last singing drunk and emptied the ashtrays and, under the eyes of the boss, poured the slops back in the barrel.

One morning while I was opening the doors, Johnny threw back a brandy and lemon, and said to me, 'Ah, listen, old cock, tonight we knock off at seven, right?'

'Right.'

'Well, you're gonna spend the night drinking with me, right? I won't *really* be there, see, but we get properly drunk, see, and then I sleep it off at your place. But I won't really be there either, ya see, I'll be somewhere else. But if anyone wants to know, like a wife or anything, I got very drunk last night and slept on the floor at your place, right?'

I slid the Pacifier underneath the counter where it could be easily reached and looked up.

'Right,' I said, 'we get drunk, but only I'm there, and then we stagger home to my place, except I'm alone.'

'Exactly, my boy. Your education wasn't wasted. Think that up yourself, did ya?'

'Yeah, just came to me in a sort of flash. Nothin' to it, really.'

I poured the first warm and headless beer for the morning's first desperate man, who drank it with a brandy, and this so impressed Johnny that he snuck out the back and had one too. Each time he had a shot he topped up the bottle with a slurp of water so that it was difficult to tell if we served the city's weakest brandy or stiffest water.

I usually had a counter tea at the pub on my night off, because Angelina the Italian lady cooked on Wednesday nights, and she liked to see nice fat boys. She piled my plate with slices of beef and roast potatoes.

I had nothing to do. My girlfriend was working, or going out with another bloke, so I polished off my tea, had a few beers, played two games of pool with long-haired Ronnie (a finder of things fallen off trucks) and settled in for the night. Johnny's scheme was fading from my mind, but I had nothing better to do than ease myself around the warm glow of drunkenness.

When it occurred to me to wonder, I imagined the dingy room behind the sandwich shop, the clothes on chairs, the sleeping child; but the fog and uproar of the pub and the stealth of an alcoholic haze were too much for my righteousness.

I can remember singing 'Barefoot Days' with old Harold, and 'Galway Bay' with Andy the Scotsman and Paddy the Irishman, but this always ended in a fight, and so I withdrew to a corner with Harold and watched as Ken the barman took off his specs and removed all the glasses and jugs from the bar. The turmoil of thistle and clover thrashed itself closer to the doorway, and with a judicious kick from long-haired Ronnie they were outside brawling in the gutter.

For every beer I bought, Ken was slipping me a free one, and I was about as primed as a Ronaldson and Tippet pump and half as effective.

Ken slipped the Pacifier across the doors and gently urged me into the street, where I found Andy crying.

'He's fallen down the drain. My stupid Irish mate has fallen down the drain!'

I could see Paddy sleeping safely on the bus-stop bench, so I patted Andy on the shoulder and assured him that Paddy probably lived down the drain.

My eyes were as heavy as lead sinkers as I walked uncertainly up Rawburn Road to catch the tram. Green and blue sparks fizzed from the power pole as the tram clattered and swayed towards me. It was as empty and bright as a laundrette, and I was quickly asleep on a wooden bench. I woke to the conductor jostling me.

'Come on, son, we've got to go home, it's late, you know.' Oh, I knew, I knew. I rubbed my eyes and stepped gingerly over the switching gear in the darkness of the terminus shed. I passed the milkman delivering milk from his cart and silent horse, and the tomcats climbing fences and sloping homeward to sleep like good pussies on pastel acrylic rugs. Here puss, puss, puss.

I had lived up to my promise. I got drunk and staggered home, and here I was opening the doors to a new day in the greyness of Rawburn. I glanced up at the bus-stop bench and walked over to peer down the stormwater drain. Paddy wasn't there, but I found Andy's shoe.

Johnny was just finishing off his first brandy when I brought in the shoe and put it on the shelf.

'What's that?' asked Johnny.

'Andy's shoe. He lost it looking for drowned Irishmen.'

'Oh,' said Johnny, with other things on his mind. 'Thanks for last night, old son. How's the head?'

'Terrific ,' I said, desperately trying to balance a brick inside my skull without it crashing through my forehead.

We closed the doors, we opened the doors, we filled glasses, they were emptied. We emptied ashtrays, they were filled. Suns and moons rose and set without our even noticing; for us it was a rhythm of open door, shut door, empty and fill.

One morning Johnny licked his lips after his first brandy and said,

'Look, old cock, I've got a favour to ask you.'

The iron bar was slid in its place, and I looked up.

'Yeah?'

'Yeah. Ya see, the missus wants to take the kids for a holiday down the beach, so I've rented this house down at Edithvale for a week. But I've got no way of getting her and the kids and all the luggage down there. The Holden isn't fixed yet – ya know the trouble I've had with me diff – so I was wondering if you'd be able to take 'em down tomorrow afternoon when ya knock off?'

He licked his lips, and his eyes went towards the brandy bottle.

'Sure,' I said, 'I could use a bit of a swim myself.'

'Good on ya, mate,' he said and clapped me on the back. 'Let's have a drink to celebrate.'

But I could hear the boss coming, so I passed Johnny a glass and towel, and we rubbed and polished as if cleanliness was our god. When the boss came in, we looked up and smiled. The jolly barmen, gleeful at their toil. Whistle while you work, and all that. We never fooled him, but he never caught us. A stalemate in a dead game.

So the morrow dawns on another sparrow dust Rawburn morning. I got into the old 1949 Morris Oxford and chugged sombrely in between the Holdens, Fords and tax-dodge Volvos to pick up my girlfriend, who was having a sickie on the strength of a day at the beach. She was young, blonde and slim and more beautiful than anything else my weekly life tossed up, and the two of us rolled around to Johnny's rented flat.

Two kids stood at a second-floor window looking down into a street beginning to bake and shimmer in the sun. On the steps I passed two bottles of souring milk and a dog chewing a blue thong. I pressed the buzzer, but it didn't buzz. When I knocked, the door was opened immediately by a boy of about ten who looked at me without expression.

'Mum!' he called, his eyes never leaving my face.

A woman appeared, wiping her hands.

'Hullo, I'm Johnny's mate. He said you needed a lift to the beach.'

'Yes, thank you very much. We're all ready. I was just cleaning up. We didn't expect you so early.'

'I'm sorry if I've come too soon – I, uh –'

'No, no, I just thought you might be held up.'

We looked at each other, and she disappeared into the room

112

and came back lugging two cases. I carried them down to the Oxford and loaded them into the boot, along with a plastic inflatable ring (Walt Disney characters) and buckets and spades (embossed with the shapes of crabs, shells and starfish).

There were beach towels, tennis balls, a game of Ludo and, if this load of holiday playthings struck me as pathetic compared with the pale face of the woman and the blankness of the children, I can't remember. I was young still, and pathos was not always recognized by my eyes.

We drove through the morning traffic and valiantly attempted to keep a conversation going. The woman talked about sunburn and cooking, and I told the boy guaranteed ways of catching flathead. I had lived most of my life by the sea and could recite the litany of sea knowledge by heart. What had happened to me since? Ah, the bright lights and grey gutters.

The beach house wasn't exactly on the beach, and the ti-tree hedge hid a very bleached little cottage stuck on the couch grass like some bone-grey driftwood from the sea.

The fraying lino and torn blinds were infecting my heart, so I drove down to the beach where we bought pies and milk shakes. Paper was blowing about the kiosk, and a change was rolling in from the sea as we laid our whipping towels on the sand.

We dumped ourselves in the water and desperately tried to appear as if we thought this was the life. The boy was the most successful; he stood thigh deep in the restless waves with his mouth agape at the gulls torn from the sky and the surf boiling on the shore. His body was thin and pale but, if his vulnerability touched my heart, I can't remember. I was young then.

I dried myself on a towel abrasive with sand and could see that Noeleen was having the same trouble with the waist of her bikini. The pale woman, nondescript in a shapeless swimsuit, was tolerating everything.

113

We left them to their beach holiday, and on the way home savoured each other's youth and unbroken hearts.

Were we in love? The juice of our lips and our palms burning with the vibrancy of each other's body made us think so. When my stomach caved to the touch of her lips on my neck, and the slide of her fingers beneath my shirt, I found my breath whispering the words we learn from the cinema darkness. I love you. I'll love you until all the stars are cold in the sky and all the rivers –.

A week later I opened the doors of the pub and heard behind me the clink of bottle on glass and Johnny said, 'The wife and kids came back with me sister-in-law last night. They had a tremendous time. Weather wasn't too good, but young Bill caught three flathead. He reckons you're the best thing since Ron Barassi.'

I was looking out on the sparrows in the gutter, and a mynah strutting bandit-eyed across the road.

'The wife is very grateful to you for taking them all down on ya day off and all. So am I, old son.'

I swept the pavement and the birds flew off.

'I've had plenty of sandwiches over the past week. I, uh, I've been living there, ya know. I'm thinking of living there all the time.'

I slid the bar out of the groove.

'I want to ask another favour of ya, old son. I want us to drink together tonight, and then sleep it off at your place like we did last time.' He eyed the Tolleys bottle. 'Ya see, I need another night to think it over, before I leave for good, I mean.' A long silence. I ran the detergent and watered beer into a jug and watched as it became darker.

'That'll be okay, Johnny,' I said, as I poured the first beers. Johnny and me were mates.

That night I ate one of Angelina's special roasts, played three games of pool with long-haired Ronnie, picked out a few horses for the Caulfield races, but declined to sing with Harold or the pride of the British Isles. The door was closed behind me, and I took a tram lit up like a ship at sea.

When I saw a phone box, I pulled the cord on the tram and jumped onto the road, waiting in the light of a shop window as a girl finished a call. She rubbed one foot against the ankle of the other and her eyes sassed at me as she giggled down the phone. 'Course I won't. No – No-o-o, don't be silly. Noooo – course not.' She kissed into the receiver, dropped the handpiece on its hook and shook back her hair. She held the door for me, her eyes wild as a pony's. I watched the quickness of her legs as she sped down the road.

The coin dropped. 'Noeleen! It's me. Me. I was going to drop by and see you. Yeah, okay, I'll bring a bottle, eh?'

The light was on in the back porch, and she opened the door before I knocked and held a finger to her lips. 'Sssh, Mum and Dad have just gone to bed.'

'You're all dressed up,' I said, pointing to her black frock.

'I've been at work. This is what the new owner wants all the waitresses to wear. Twenty dollars in tips tonight, so I don't mind.' She reached her arms around my neck and kissed me under the ear. One strap of her dress slid off her white shoulder. She held my head as I took the nipple between my lips and let the weight of her breast fill the centre of my palm. I knew there were tears in my eyes.

So slow she was. Arching, she brought me to the back of a warm cave, held me there, drew me back, held me again. I was losing my eyes, my temples seemed frail and translucent as Japanese screens. I held her up with one hand, pressed myself to her, and before she cried out I was trembling, shivering with rippling spasms.

I stared at stripes of dull light made by the Venetian blinds, stared for hours until I became aware of the thrown tableau of our limbs, her breathing, her quiet hand on my nape.

That night I dreamt of two perfectly white birds flying above the sea against a perfectly blue sky. They wheeled and plunged after each other as I had seen two Pacific herons do. One hazy, seductive circle after another. And then, in the dream, it was me in the sky quietly falling towards the sea, unafraid. I was holding the back of a plain wooden chair, and it rested gently in the shallow sea, and my feet were in the warm aqua water, treading sand crimped like the roof of a mouth.

I woke walking through these mild shallows towards the most perfectly scooped beach.

I drank a glass of water in the kitchen, leaning against the sink. My whole body was suffused with the ascent from the dream and the memory of two bodies joined by the warm cups and buds of their centres. The peach stone and bed of soft flesh.

And I thought of Johnny and the pale woman and children, the sandwich woman, her child. There was no connection with my life, surely. No doubt could have withstood my blind intent, no sturdy voice could dissuade me from the pursuit of that ascent, even if only once more. My eyes had no sight. Not blind, but my blood refused any other function than that expiation of everything on earth. I couldn't deny the censer and the dark vault.

Next morning I drew the bar and pushed open the door on another train-clattering day, and there she was with her pale face and wispy dark hair. I held to the iron bar and swallowed.

'G'day. How was the beach?'

'Was he with you last night?'

'Yeah. Ah – we had a few beers.'

'Will he leave me?'

What do I say? I thought, clinging to the bar and hearing footsteps behind me recede to the back bar. The clink of glass.

'Well, will he?'

'I don't know what –'

'You weren't with him last night. I know where he was – all I want to know is, will he leave me?'

'I – uh –'

'Will he go with her?'

'I don't – I hope –' She turned away from my stammering. I

stepped away from the door and reached to her with my voice.
'I'll speak to him – I'll tell him –'

She turned back to look at me. 'Do you love that girl?' I
thought of the night and the joy of our tangled bodies and the
whispered promises.

'I don't know,' I said, and we looked at each other, and I saw
the brittle dullness of her hair and eyes, and she saw the apple-
bloom of my cheeks.

'Neither did I,' she said.

# *NAUTILUS*

*F*rom the window of the Gellibrand house you could see far out across the ocean. A bitter draught of winter had interrupted spring and sent hard pellets of rain stinging across the windows, and wind tearing at the house and the dunes. The grey-green sea roared, foam flying from its howling crests.

Helen sat in the bay window searching the ocean with binoculars, and far out at sea she saw the whale surfacing in a rhythmic arch, spouting, heedless of the chill of thrashing water, oblivious to the bleakness others saw in its world. Her eyes strained through the lenses and she imagined the bleating of the whales as they coursed that desolate sea.

She remembered the bleak corridors and sterile kitchens and the nights when she had lain awake listening to other women whimpering in their sleep. She remembered praying. To get out. She remembered a bench in the cool of the summer evening, voices murmuring with the crickets, the pittosporum perfume and slowly wheeling stars. When she stood up to leave, he had stood with her, wishing her goodnight, touching her elbow with his fingertips.

A log fire burnt behind her and on the wood stove a kettle.

Outside the forest brooded beneath the battering of the storm. The mug of coffee warmed her hands, but nothing could warm the eyes that scanned the cold water world of the whale, the beast that searched and sieved the sea, conscious of the smallest things.

In the afternoon she walked the streets of the town. Her coat was huge and heavy, and she huddled inside it. She walked along the shore, small dotterels skittering before her, the sand pocked with rain. The sea surged in great chaotic collapses of towering water.

Gouts of seaweed teemed with lice, and abalone torn from their rock lay stranded on the beach beside bloating toadfish and marker buoys lost at sea.

At the end of the beach, where a claw of rock probed grimly into the sea, she found a seal washed up among the kelp and driftwood. It watched her approach with a steady but frantic eye and tried to lift itself on its flippers. Helen, swaddled in her great coat, stood over the beast, searching her mind for her child's-encyclopaedia knowledge of seals, trying to discover how to save its life. She stood helpless above the animal that looked back at her with a mixture of grief, malevolence and despair.

That night she entered her familiar dream world; her lips were about to touch those of a man dressed wholly in black. As she reached forward she found herself kissing the salty beak of a seal. The seal didn't resist but allowed her to kiss him. He had the small eye of sea things – the eye of the lost at sea.

In the morning she drank coffee in the garden, throwing pieces of bread to a shrike thrush. The day was becoming warmer, and Helen walked to the beach, her feet bare on the gravel. The dream was leaving her, and her heart was gladdened by the seagulls bucking in the bright air. She even waved to the woman at the store.

Mrs Pritchard returned her greeting, and sidled towards Mr Talbot, who was cleaning the winter windows of his fishing tackle shop. 'That's Dr Goding's daughter, Mr Talbot. Remember the little girl who played the piano that night over at May Thompson's Christmas Eve party. She's been sick, you know. The doctor's wife asked me to keep an eye on her, make sure she's all right.' They watched her walking up the street.

'Been very sick, so they say. Nerves. Mrs Thompson says you can tell.'

'Funny, that,' Mr Talbot said, squeezing soapsuds from his window. Mrs Pritchard left, and he stared into the window where landing nets, rods, reels and the gimcrack gadgetry of holiday fishing prepared to lure cod-faced tourists.

On the beach she found the frail parchment nautilus shell, the ribbed and horned sail shell, still whole after travelling an ocean that had snapped ships' cables and torn anchors from their clawhold on the rocky bottom.

She held the shell in her palm and deep inside she could see a blush of flesh-pink. The perfect spiral of the shell left a great peace in her heart. She set it secure in the sand pointed towards the sea, and lay down beside it, letting the slow metronome of the surf buoy her far across the water. Borne like a nautilus, unharmed, a mermaid gleaming with shimmering scales and streaming hair.

'Hullo.' She opened her eyes to find a man gazing down at her. They sat together looking out to sea. Helen told him about the whale she had seen, and together they examined the nautilus. Her hair draped over his wrist as she leant to show him the fragile pinkness in the innermost part of the shell. His eyes dilated as he half listened to her explanation of the shell, his whole being engrossed in the sensation of the flow of her hair across his hand and arm. She became expansive and told him again of the storms and the birds she fed, and even about Mrs Pritchard's knick-knackery store and stale biscuits. She was enthusiastic like a child, and her excitement kindled his own. Her description of the postmaster's bifocals and the precarious perching of these spectacles on the old man's nose seemed hilarious.

Helen brushed the sand from her hair and his old jumper, then stopped with her hand on his shoulder, examining the stitches.

'Peter, it's Tuesday, isn't it?'

'Wednesday!' he replied.

'Wednesday! You should be at work. How did you know where I was?'

He slid his hands inside the veil of her hair, and clasped her neck. He was about to speak, but she pressed two fingers against his lips and turned her face away.

'Come on!' she said, and began pulling at his arms to lift him.

They walked along the beach of wheeling gulls and skittering dotterels. She wondered at his selflessness, his acceptance, the way he didn't press himself upon her. Every time she looked at his face she could see a crumpling of flesh around the eyes, but the eyes themselves, although dark and tightened with the sutures of pain, were bright at their centre, ready, wanting to laugh.

Peter walked ahead and stood over a dark hulk on the sand. The eye that had searched and pleaded was gone, taken as a lush oyster by a hook-beaked skua. Lice boiled in the crater.

As they trudged up the street between the shops, watched between the tackle by Mr Talbot and across tins of soup by Mrs Pritchard, and over his spectacles by the postmaster, they walked arm in arm to the bone-grey weatherboard house that hunched like sea wrack at the foot of the rainforest.

'Must be that husband of hers,' said Mr Talbot as he turned the key in his door. Mrs Pritchard, pulling up her canvas blind, narrowed her eyes, and her lips became taut.

'I've seen her husband, and that's not him,' she said, and stalked inside and shut her door. Mr Talbot was left in the street holding his dangling keys and looking from the starchy departure of Mrs Pritchard to the couple dawdling up the street, their shoulders bumping together.

'Funny that,' mused Mr Talbot, pocketing his keys and turning for home, his mind letting the vision of Mrs Pritchard and the lovers become a plate of Cape Cod placed before him by his tea-caddy wife.

'Look,' said Peter, 'I'll get us something to eat, will I?' He looked at her quickly.

'No, no, I'll cook tea for you. There's plenty of food. The cupboards are full. I'll never get through it all . . .'

Mrs Pritchard, aware of his approach, continued to place the huge hasp on her door.

'Excuse me, I'm sorry I'm late, but I need some groceries. There's nothing in the house.'

'I'm just shutting,' said Mrs Pritchard, holding up the huge lock and poised key as evidence.

'Yes, I can see that,' said Peter, 'but I would really appreciate just a couple of minutes to get some things for tea.'

Mrs Pritchard made a great show of unlocking her shop. She put goods on the counter, and fixed him with a bright eye.

'Staying around here, are you?'

'Oh yes, yes, just for the day.'

'Oh,' she said, tallying the prices and adding a bit for disapproval.

'Got friends here, have you?'

'Yes, friends.'

Helen left the piano and helped him with the parcels.

'I don't think your lady at the store approves of me,' said Peter, searching for an opener.

'Well, you're not my husband, are you. Everybody knows everybody else's business down here.'

They raised their glasses to each other and sighed for the first clean draught of cold beer.

'What are you doing?' asked Peter, glancing at the piano.

'I'm writing a story of seals and whales, and of this.' She tapped the glass case where she had placed the nautilus shell.

'You're writing music?' He looked at her. She moved to the piano and began to play.

He sat at the window looking across the darkening ocean, where the foam of the waves was a snowy iridescence on the shore. The music was the ocean he gazed upon and he wasn't aware that the keys had stopped until he felt her hands on his shoulders.

Mr and Mrs Talbot slept belly to bum, a congestion of pyjama cords and cotton. Her hand held an arm below the shoulder; his hand held a book closed upon his thumb.

Mrs Pritchard had her problems with a pattern, and crimped wool coiled at her feet awaiting the clarification of maths.

The postmaster really did like stamps, and wore a regulation eyeshade as he scanned sheets of stamps for kangaroos without tails, wrens with three legs, and cross-eyed princesses. His wife stood hands on hips, staring at the slow stewing of quince jam, daring it not to clear.

Water rats held sweet mussels between their paws and watched for owls. Owls blinked and watched for rats; and wombats watched out for themselves.

Surf and heartbeats were the great metronomes for them all. All of them in time to their own quiet night breathing, paced by darkness.

Dawn bathed Helen's room, gilding the bodies enmeshed in each other's arms, drowned in the nets of love, beach-washed on slow waves.

They sat on a bench in the sun, eating green apples and grapes. The thrush cocked his head, and the magpie carolled in the high limbs.

'What do we do now?' she asked, watching the thrush hop to her feet.

He didn't look up.

'What do we do about the rest? Your wife, my husband, your kids?'

'Yes, the kids.'

She grasped his hand. 'Peter, I don't want to go back . . .'

Helen walked the beach, and where the river entered the sea she found a shattered nautilus shell, the pale flesh-pink of the spirals exposed to the scrabbling claws of the crabs and hook-billed gulls. She knelt above the shell but withdrew her hands, resisting the temptation to play jigsaws. The beach was littered with remnants that the sea spat up.

She selected the spiral core of the shell and dropped it in her pocket, and turned from the sea.

# *SOLDIER GOES TO GROUND*

*I*t was a paddy field that had been slurped into mush, like a huge plate of baby cereal. And they were firing at him. He didn't want to be killed. He didn't want to feel the scorch of hot metal rip through his tissues. As he ran, he could imagine the lead searching to plunge a hole through his back. His spine tingled as he slushed through the mud and blasted harvest.

There was a lump, a sodden thing, and he fell beside it, hiding his head. He panted into his arm, his body sinking into the sour mud. The firing continued, but nothing found a cave of flesh, at least not his flesh. He opened his eyes and saw that his shelter wore a uniform, the same uniform, and that the intestines were beginning to stray from beneath the jacket. They were a puzzle, a mystery, an organic jigsaw.

He couldn't be sick. He couldn't be sad. He had his own warm sack of tubes to protect from the blazing hounds of the air. What were they firing at? He seemed to have been here for hours. Surely the others were all gone, or dead, like this fallen lump he hid behind. He dared not lift his head. Perhaps they assumed he was dead. He let his face sink deeper into the

125

slush, wishing that the mud would embrace him, take him into its arms and protect him.

'G'day.' Silence punctuated by bursts of fire. 'Rather be at Lorne, meself.' Who spoke? Involuntarily, he lifted his head an inch and swivelled his eyes to look around. No one, only the corpse, and then he saw the eyes looking at him.

'Give you a fright, did I? You'd better stick your head down again, mate. You can stay here until it stops. I don't think I'm going anywhere.'

His eyes slewed to the side to look at the mess of gut seeping from beneath the jacket, and he felt ashamed of the glance, but the corpse had seen the direction of his gaze.

'I know. I tried to put it back, but I can't move any more. I can't even feel it any more. Like a bad dream, except it's not, is it?'

'Can I do –'

'No, I don't think so.' The dead and living gazed at each other across eight inches of mud.

'There is one thing you can do for me, in return for a bit of shelter.' A sick green smile stretched the facial muscles of the spoilt soldier.

'There's something in my top pocket, and I want you to give it to someone in Melbourne.' A sodden silence.

'Take it for me.' The living soldier watched in dismay as a bead of moisture fled the cheek of the face that was taking on the texture of an old sago pudding.

'Give it to a girl who lives at 46 Pacific Street, Brunswick. Sue.'

The breath was still stirring the puddle between their faces, but the eyes had closed. The lips parted jerkily once more, but no sound came, and the pool of slush became still.

He stared for an age at the white-green mask, before he saw his fingers grappling with the button of the top pocket. These fingers disappeared and withdrew a shell, a frail pink shell. In acres of slop and screaming air, two fingers held a perfect shell.

Pacific Street. Pacific Street. Forty, forty-eight, forty-six. Brunswick. Brunswick. In the hardly credible world away from this rice bowl, there was Brunswick, a casual half-hour drive from his own home.

The sky began to turn an acrid yellow as sunset became soured with the smoke of shellfire and marsh haze. The last shots were fired, and two pucked into the back of the sheltering corpse and kicked it like a baker might casually thump a bag of flour. A dull, thick sound.

Shell, shells. Shell, shells. He slunk away from the curdling sack of guts, bearing with him the shell. An eye for an eye. A shell for a shell.

Life was best lived in a daze. Not a stupor, but a coma of the softer parts of the mind. The bits for running, preserving, drinking and eating could continue unimpaired, while the other senses crouched away from the bodies falling or bleeding, the gaping faces of mothers and children, the flames, the ruined fields, the spoilt soldiers in threshed fields of grain. Discarded sacks of life. As wasteful and careless as a sackful of kittens in a sewer.

But he ran and hid, drank and ate, and nothing punctured his frail consciousness and nothing pierced his warm bag of flesh until one day he saw a boy's face appear between leaves. There was a flash, and he almost *saw* it coming for his leg. The child was terrified and had hardly aimed at all. But ten others aimed at the boy, and his pouch of life was penetrated and then left to bloat like a cow – or a calf.

He watched in amazement from starchy sheets as infection grew and the sag-eyed doctors stood around, lifting the sheet to look, to glance at each other, and finally to send him home.

And to be sure, there was a bit missing out of his leg, but it healed perfectly. The boy in the bushes had sent him a ticket for home and paid for it. Dearly.

\* \* \*

127

Pacific Street, Brunswick. He stepped from the car and walked in suburban street sunshine to the terrace with 46 screwed to the mortar. The door knocked hollow. It opened and a girl looked out at him, inquiringly.

'Does a girl called Sue live here?'

'Yes, she's inside. I'm Brenda. Come in.'

Brenda sashayed into the kitchen. 'Suzanne, there's a man to see you.'

'Hullo. I, I knew a friend of yours. Could I speak to you privately?' Brenda whistled between her teeth.

'Wow, what a smoothie!' Brenda saw his eyes as she spoke, and left the room swiftly.

'I was in Penang and I met this man, and he gave me your address and a present for you, and he died before he could say . . . His name was Ken Simpson.'

Suzanne drew on a cigarette and stared at the man before her. She pressed the butt into an ashtray.

'Look, oh look, I'm sorry, but I only moved here two months ago. The other girl before me, she was called Sue. I'm Suzanne. Sue's gone to Sydney with – I'm really sorry. Look, sit down and I'll get you a cup of coffee.'

She clanked the kettle on to the stove and tossed spoons of coffee into mugs.

'Was he a friend of yours?' The soldier looked up from his hands.

'No, well, I'd only just met him.' She held a cup of coffee towards him.

'Was that the present?' she asked as she nodded towards the shell in his hands.

'Yes, he didn't say what –'

They drank the silence from their coffee cups and, though his face was averted, she could tell he was crying, the shell twisting in his hands. He turned to her.

'I'm sorry, it's not the shell or anything. I hardly, I only knew him for a few minutes, but for the first time –'

She'd seen enough Rock Hudson films to know that this is

what soldiers do when they come home. And there was always a Florence Nightingale to apply the soft hand and soothing words.

'Look, we're having a party on here tonight. Why don't you stay around and join in?' Brenda entered the room and saw the soldier looking crumpled and Suzanne's hand on his shoulder.

Suzanne glanced at her friend. 'This man, he knew one of Sue's boyfriends, it seems, and came to give her a present. We haven't even got her Sydney address, have we? What was that Stewart fella's name? We might be able to look that up in the phone book. Anyway, I've invited him to the party.' Suzanne nodded to indicate the soldier.

She brought him wine and cheeses while she tidied the house and made plates of food. He watched through the window the last sun on terrace walls turning the street into a flat facade. She filled his wineglass again and he allowed himself to drop behind the aquarium with its lonely goldfish. People came and went around him. The party spread and grew, dividing carefully around his chair.

The music washed up against the glass in front of his face, and the dancers were like weeds moving in the water.

'Hey mate, this yours?' A shell was held over his face, and he reached up from the deep and took it, slipped it into his pocket. I'd rather be in Lorne.

He woke with sun creeping across his eyes, and he stared at the window, waiting to know where he was.

Pacific Street, 46, Brunswick. There was a body behind him, its arm flung across his neck. He reached back and touched the skin. Warm. His hand followed the curve of hip and thigh, and he turned his head. The eye was looking at him.

'Sleep?'

'Must have.'

She reached across him and picked up the shell from a table and held it for him to see.

'I saved your shell. You started yelling a bit.'

'Did I?'

'Mmmm. About Lorne. If you keep it up they might make you mayor.' She ran a hand round the scoop of his waist and over his belly, and the tingling of his vulnerability was like pain. Sharp as blades.

'Dearly beloved,' the minister half yelled into the wind. This was the first time he had heard the soldier of shelter's name. The family looked at him, but after the service had turned to shepherd the mother from the grave. He was left in the wind and the sour smell of clay. His coat flapped at his legs and blew hair back from his face. He leant forward and dropped the shell into the grave.

'Friend of yours, son?' His heart leapt. People were forever creeping up and talking at him. His heart slowed down and he turned to see the man with the spade.

'A friend.'

'Very sorry, mate.' The shoveller was waiting to shovel.

At the iron gates of the cemetery he pushed his hands into his pockets, and the fingers involuntarily searched the linings before he turned his eyes to look up the street.

'Bunch of flowers, sir.' Christ! he thought, and pushed money at her before she could speak again. He pressed the marigolds to his stomach and hurried up the street.

'Flowers!' she said, and he held them out to her. She brought the yellow and gold to her face and looked at him, wondering about the next move, the next word. The trip wires and triggers, shelters and tombs. Neither of them spoke across the marigolds.

# *SIRENS*

*I*t was windy on the pier. It usually is. He sat on a bollard watching his mother who was sitting on the edge of the pier beside the kiosk.

Her shoes were as bright red as her lips, but the wind seemed not to bother her hair, as it did the other fishermen who huddled in stained fishing gear.

She held her rod delicately in front of her and, whereas the others were surrounded by crushed mussels and bags spilling prawns and white bait, she was accompanied only by a black handbag.

Kevin shifted from the bollard and walked along the pier.

'Hullo, Mum.' Her face was a neat mask, and when she saw her son it didn't change. The red lips parted, but there was a silence before she spoke.

'Hullo.'

'Did you get my card? I've come down to see you, Mum.' He watched his mother's face with interest. Not desperate interest, but interest anyway. Her reaction was important to him, and so he waited. She was quietly doing something with the line, and he watched passively.

'I got the card. I put it on the shelf.' He waited. It wasn't a panicky wait; he hadn't seen his mother for six years. He watched and waited with the air of a wised-up youth who took an interest in things. Nothing mattered much, but he wanted to know anyway.

She had reeled in the line, and now she studied the prawn on the hook. Clearly she wasn't going to say anything further. He shifted his weight from one leg to the other as he squatted beside her.

'I thought I might stay in the house for a couple of days, have a look around again, just for a couple of days, you know. If it was okay with you, I mean, I wanted to see how you were. Here, I brought you something from Sydney.' He handed her one of those little glass domes. In this one gold flecks were settling on the sails of the Sydney Opera House.

She took her eyes from the dome and placed it gently in her pocket. 'Thanks, Kevin.' It was probable that it would go beside the card on the mantelpiece, together with the bright-red department store alarm clock, an arrangement of dried flowers and a small statue of a Japanese girl dressed in a kimono.

The woman stood with the rod in one hand and the bag in the other. 'I'm going back now.' There was a pause as she looked at her reel as if there might be a tangle in the line. 'Are you staying for tea?'

'Yes,' he said, preparing to walk beside her. 'Yes, I thought I'd stay for a couple of days, Mum.' He was walking beside her. The other fishermen sat dangling their legs over the side or sitting on small canvas stools. No one was catching anything, and the wind tore words off lips before they could reach any listener's ear. So all the fishermen sat silent in their coats as the wind flicked their hair in their eyes.

In Grey Street the first girls were settling into their beat in a half-hearted way. Most of them spoke to the woman as she passed. 'Hullo, Ruby, how are things? Okay?' Then they stared suspiciously at the young stranger who walked by her side. The woman answered these greetings by lifting her gaze from the street and opening and closing her lips. You could see that her red lips formed the shape of a name each time, but it was not certain whether any sound left them.

They arrived at a small, black gate in a low brick fence just as some more girls came out of the door of the boarding house. The same greetings took place.

They walked up the stairs, and she unlocked the door to a small room. She put on the kettle, took off her coat and glanced once at the mirror. He sat in an old wicker chair by the window, and looked around the room he knew. His eyes rested on the mantelpiece where his mother was placing the gift beside the card, the clock and the exquisite doll. Gold flecks settled once again on the sails of the Opera House.

Over a cup of tea he began to tell her about his life in Sydney, about his job at the dairy, about where he lived in Newtown, his mates, the Opera House. A police siren wailed and was gone. Both listened to it, waiting with practised attention.

He began to ask about other people he had known here when he was sixteen. To each query she gave a brief account. Police, death, pregnancy or disappearance figured in nearly all the lives of the people who had formed the background to his childhood.

'One-legged Jimmy, what happened to him?'

'Jimmy?' The woman stared into the unlit gas fire. 'Jimmy went away last winter. No one knows where he is.'

'What about Shirley, you know, Vera's kid?'

'Shirley works over at Balaclava, and old Vera died. Shirley came back for the funeral.'

'What about Janice, you know, Janice who started to work here just before I went to Sydney.' The boy leaned a little further towards his mother. Perhaps the boy's interest didn't escape the woman in the chair. 'Janice is still here. She had a baby, I think. Yes, she did, but it's not here now. I think Pam down the road is looking after it, or maybe it went to a home. Janice still works here. We passed her coming home this afternoon.' The boy almost asked which one, but didn't.

The conversation ended when the boy could think of no more people to ask about. The woman began to cook sausages on a stove in the corner of the room. The boy looked around. The room was old and badly painted, but it was neat and, despite the cooking, smelt better than the rest of the house where a mixture of feline and human urine dampened the back of the nostrils. For all he knew, dark carpeted halls always had that smell.

His mother fascinated him. Perhaps fascinated is the wrong word. His mother interested him. In his memory she had always remained distinct from her background. Even when she was working, before she became the boarding-house cleaner, she had an air of scrupulous tidiness. He could vaguely remember her passing the door once or twice on her way down the corridor in company with some furtive man. But she was always different from the others and everyone in the area treated her with a little special courtesy. Just a fraction more kindness and regard, even politeness.

He wondered about her. Almost without speaking (it was incredible, but he could hardly remember her ever speaking) she had encouraged, or was it willed him to stay at school for those extra couple of years. It could hardly be called a conscious desire, but it had come about. He remembered noticing an air of satisfaction about her shoulders and the top of her head as she looked down at his final report. He knew she couldn't read it, but equally he knew she was pleased. In this house, a Form Four certificate was a mark of success.

He finished his tea and watched as she made up his old bed in the corner near the fireplace. He lit a cigarette and smoked as his mother washed the dishes.

'I think I'll just go for a bit of a walk, Mum. I'll see you later.'

He leant on the verandah rail looking out into the street where the groups of girls stood at each corner or lounged on the garden fences of the other boarding-houses. Old red brick warrens with names from the past when this was a fashionable resort. Kia-Ora, Gladeside Mews, Orana, Dutson Terrace, Philby Lodge. All of them, now, boarding-house warrens with dark, dank halls.

Girls passed him as they went out into the street and others as they entered with a furtive or squalid man. The furtive ones were always well dressed, the squalid ones were always drunk. All glanced suspiciously at the young man leaning against the verandah rail. A fattish woman of about forty came up the path towards the front door, glanced at the youth and stopped.

'Kevin! 'Ullo, Kevin love, come back to see ya mum, 'ave ya?'

'That's right, Flo,' he said as the woman swamped his shoulders with her heavy arm. 'How are things with you, Flo?' She pulled away and flung an arm around in a hopeless gesture. 'Ar, you know how things are around here, Kev - up and down!' She winked suddenly and huge gusts of laughter burst from her chest. He waited until she had stopped shaking and asked, 'Have you seen Janice around tonight?'

'Janice, yes, yes, she's just down the road there, down at Gipps Street.'

'Thanks, Flo, I'll go and have a yarn with her. See you around, Flo.'

He saw two women standing on the corner but they were both blonde and had their backs to him, and he couldn't see which was Janice.

'Hello, Janice,' he said. She turned and recognized him immediately and saw how he struggled to see in her face the girl he had known. 'Hello, Kevin, it's good to see you again. Down for a while, are you?'

'Yes, couple of days. What about a drink later on?'

'Sure, that'd be great. Come around to my room about twelve, okay?' Pour yourself a drink and make yourself comfortable if I'm not there, I won't be long. She gave him a smile that had the left-over traces of forced seductiveness. Her face became blank as she searched his face.

135

He lay on her bed drinking beer in the half-light of a hooded lamp, listening to the blare of sirens that crept through the window from streets all over St Kilda. They were hardly ever silent. Sometimes faint and far off down near Luna Park, at other times close by in Fitzroy Street, and when they cruised past in Grey Street he lay rigid in bed with half his face lit by the bed lamp, silent and listening.

When Janice came in he poured her a beer. She lay back on the bed and threw an arm across her eyes to shield them from the light in the room and the glow of the city that cast ghostly sheets of light between the curtains.

They talked of their friends and school, and in his eyes she could see the reflection of the extent of change in herself. She sighed and passed a gassy breath of beer and stared at the ceiling.

'You should see Sydney, Janice.' He leaned on an elbow, looking down at her, pushed the hair from her forehead and traced the brow. Her eyes were shut.

'You should see it, it's terrific. The beaches and the bridge, all the rivers and that. You'd love it up there. I'm livin' in the Ship Inn right under the bridge. Right under it.' He looked down at her again and her eyes stared back.

'It's nothin' to make five hundred a week up there. Pull a few beers, cart a bit of furniture, win a bit on the nags. Sell a bit of dope.' He looked down at her again and saw the easy rise and fall of her chest, her face turned to his arm .

'Easy up there. Me and a mate go surfin' at Bondi nearly every day. Hop on the train and Bob's yer uncle. Better waves than here. St Kilda's a bloody drain compared to Bondi. You'd love it up there. We could get a place out near the Junction.'

His hand smoothed the hair and slipped along her shoulder and breast, waist and thigh. She hooked an arm around his neck and breathed against him, holding him, drawing him to her. She was asleep almost immediately, and the lines around her eyes relaxed. The glow of city-light made her face lunar-white. Single strands of hair shone as they spread across his chest. He watched her face become beautiful, while the sirens sang on the Rocks.

Occasionally a brass laugh shook the walls next door and once the smash of glass was heard downstairs, and still she slept against him. He spread her hair out over his belly, and still the sirens called. Down in the street there were raised voices and finally a crash, and someone moaning. He could imagine the blood and the staggering of the man stumbling against the fences, holding his face. Once again the house was quiet.

A siren slurred to a stop. There was a running in the corridor, a door slammed against a wall. He lay rigid, waiting, his hand resting on the hair that shone so in the night. He couldn't bring himself to move, to stir the sleeping girl-woman, to remove from the light her golden head.

The door was flung open, light slashed and a young policeman covered him with a gun. An older man entered the room. 'Hullo, Kevin. Sorry to disturb you.' The detective stepped into the room and glanced about, taking in the poverty and the two gilded lovers. 'It's the money, Kevin, You'd better get up.' He indicated Janice with one finger, even he seemed reluctant to wake her. Kevin tried to ease Janice back onto the pillow, but she woke and saw immediately. 'Christ, you bastards! Can't you leave us alone?' She began to cry, and Kevin noticed how her hair hung against her shoulders and along the curve of her arm, but they were leading him down the hall. His mother stood by the mantel-piece scanning the faces of all three men.

The older policeman leant on the mantelpiece and played with the glass bubble. He was watching the woman's face. He gave the bubble a flick and just touched the woman's shoulder as he turned to look at the boy. There was a tightness around his lips as he spoke. 'See you, Ruby.'

She heard them leave and watched as the last gold speck settled on the Opera House as sirens called from all the street corners.

# GRAVITY AND LEVITY

*E*verything hangs down. Eventually. Take a woman's breasts, for instance. There they are at eighteen, high and arrogant with their alert new horizontal growth. Five years later the lift is starting to go down. Going down, please.

Feel the flesh under your own neck, thought Partridge, or the skin beneath your eyes. If you've been exposed to the gravitational pull of our globe for sufficient time, you'll notice that the skin is trying to leave your bones. A man's hair will come out, but when it does it will fall down. Tears will creep beside your nose and then plop, down. When people die, they go straight down like a stone. Same with dogs after a bus has passed too close.

And hyacinths. The obscene green sheath strikes up out of the soil, all succulent erotic growth, blooms in a crowd of perfumed blue, and then one day you notice a blackening of the petals and right before your eyes it's dead, prostrate in a matter of days. Gravity.

Now levity. Take any kid with a ball, and he'll throw it up. Buy the kid a helium balloon and before you've left Luna Park, the kid'll let it go to pick his nose, and there she goes. A balloon rising over the beach. Rising, rising, closely followed by the kid's uplifted howl.

Take any balcony at midnight on a clear evening. A man steps out of the party to the balcony and immediately looks up to the stars, and his cigarette smoke will make pathetic attempts to shroud the moon. The man will stare at the sky, his soul reaching out from the discomfort of his suit, trying to turn the universe into a page of *Cole's Funny Picture Book*. When he fails, chances are he'll look down at the street below and experience the sensation of tipping and falling, imagining his body stamped on the footpath between the Toyotas. Not by his own despair but by gravity. Partridge remembered a few such nights on balconies.

Dingoes are even worse, he thought. The dog that cannot bark can still manage a howl and it's always up. The neck is stretched, and the voice is projected towards the moon. The same beseeching howl up at the night. The same dog shot by the bullet of a farmer doing the right thing by primary industry and the export drive will at first leap in the air, but it's only a momentary ascension of the soul, because then, plump, there's the body on the ground. Even the bullets of righteousness are on a downward curve as soon as they leave the barrel.

When a body dies, the mourners and priests lift their voices and appeal to heaven, but they always put the body in the ground.

But we try. Notre Dame, for instance. The fairytale spires are built as delicately as icing trinketry, and inside choirs conspire to give the illusion that their voices are reaching all the way to heaven. You look up, and the leaping vaults of the cathedral draw your soul, make you think for a moment that yes, yes. But then your foot scrapes against something; you bend and pick up a piece of the ceiling. A lump of blue plaster with the foot of a cherub painted on it. A piece of icing has fallen off the cake. You feel like Henny Penny.

A moonlit night on a lake in the wilderness. You paddle

along the moonshine's beam, and it's like a staircase. A yellow brick road. You paddle on, on, surely you're rising, lifted by the moonbeam's gauze to heaven. But you're not. The canoe strikes a reef of sharp oysters, and you sink, slowly. Gravity.

When you travel across the equator for the first time, your friends will race you upstairs and fill the bath and pull out the plug and point. See, the water goes the other way! This is what you've flown across the world to see, but it's a sham. It's no different. The water still goes down. That's the only direction of significance. A juggler knows he's lost his touch when there are more oranges on the ground than in the air. This is the way Partridge had been looking at things. When he saw the milk-white bum of his wife's lover leap off her when Partridge opened the door, it was a grave situation, but it only touched him with its levity. He was looking at things the wrong way. To pray was tempting, but the knowledge that prayers go up and the person who prays stays down and is preyed upon encouraged him to avoid aspiration.

He was a journalist. A good journalist. At the top of his – He groaned. Here he was interviewing a character for the features page. Good Saturday morning reading. The man was a busker. A one-man band. Partridge could see all the angles: the depression had forced them all out onto the streets in droves of violins, mouth organs and white-faced jugglers – with more oranges down than up.

But this bloke had been at it all his life. A string on his heel made a stick beat the drum on his back, his hands played an accordion, his elbow clashed an opposing cymbal tied to his belt, and he blew a mouth organ rigged in front of his face. If anyone looked at him while he played, he stopped and held out his cupped hand, and his face made the shape of that almost noiseless mewling cry that kittens make. The mouth opens, beseeching, pathetic – almost noiseless.

But he was a character. Good reading. Perhaps the subject of a journalists' award. Partridge asked the man about his busking. Had he been forced onto the streets by unemployment. The man said no, making the same face as the kitten. Disconcerting. Well, had he been a famous music hall performer who had been – The man said no. Well, the songs, then – were they his own compositions? No. He only played 'Apple Blossom Time'. 'Apple Blossom Time' – all the time? No wonder nobody put much into his hand. It didn't sound anything like 'Apple Blossom Time', Partridge thought as he folded his notebook, defeated. If the busker could indicate to people the name of the noise he was making he'd do much better. Every second American he passed, at least. Partridge opened his mouth to suggest it, but the one-man band was banging, squeezing, clanging and blowing up the mall.

At Luna Park he realized he'd done it all before. The bored men on the merry-go-rounds had told their stories to him before. Their tales of circus caravan fires, falls off the tightrope, maulings by lions, and finally the end of the line: the merry-go-round at Luna Park. That had made a good read on a Saturday morning.

He'd interviewed the woman in the take-away stall too, and as he passed he waved his hand, as she seemed to be waving at him. But he saw that she only had fairy floss on her fingers and was trying to flick it off. He noticed that even the candy gossamers gradually drifted down.

Then he saw the man on the tower about to dive into the tiny tub of water. When enough people had gathered, whoosh! down he came like a stone. Splash. He surfaced with coins between his teeth. One of the coins that bystanders had thrown into the tub to tempt the high diver back to earth. Here was a story, here was a character. Bet his wife didn't have lovers with white, querulous bums.

Partridge watched as the man in his spangled neck-to-knee Speedos climbed the ladder. Up, up, up. Partridge strained his neck as the high diver cleared the background of tents, ferris wheels and frantic flags, and etched himself against the blue as sharp as acid on a coin.

The diver spread his arms and tipped forward, but Partridge

turned away and scrambled through the crowd. He knew the diver was coming down. Even after the magnificent ascension. Even after that heraldic pose it was only playing at rising above the ordinary plane. The ladder he had climbed had been bought secondhand from the fire department. It had seen a thousand buildings burn down in laughing flames.

He pushed himself clear of the crowd and his ears burned, listening backwards for the splash as his mind hurried his body out of range. He could never remember the splash afterwards. If it ever came –

'Mr Partridge –'

'Yes.'

'How are you today?'

'Fine. Very well. Top of the –'

'Now, now, Mr Partridge, don't make that face. You look like someone's cat left out in the cold. We thought you'd like to see the film today. Most of the other patients have seen "The Holy Grail", but we thought you could do with some cheering up.'

'Up?'

'Yes, why not? No point staying miserable all the time. You're an intelligent man, Mr Partridge, a top journalist, but you seem to spend too much time letting things get you down. It's about time you bucked up a bit.'

So he sat in the hospital theatrette in his dressing gown, fiddling with the stupid fly on his pyjama pants. A scientific world, sending men to the moon, and we can't design pyjama pants with flies that stay done up. Up! Oh Jesus –

He was in a panic by the time they started the shorts. It began with a lampoon of Christmas cards. When they shot the deer out of the snowy Christmas scene, and it plopped down on the snow, with its blood turning the whiteness pink, he stood up and gripped the edges of the chair, but when they started singing 'On the First Day of Christmas' he knew they were going to shoot the partridge out of the pear tree, and he rushed at the projectionist mindless of his flapping fly. They grappled on the floor in a whorl of 16 mm film. The Siemens on its side was still churring away happily, projecting a flotilla of gondolas on the threshing bodies.

Finally he was in a ward by himself, tucked into bed with wide belts. That night he dreamt that he was watching a man in a white robe climbing a ladder. It was a fireman's ladder and cruelly truncated. An awful insult to the nature of the white-robed figure's mission. He was climbing, climbing, climbing, always looking up, apparently unaware that there were only three rungs to go.

Partridge was bellowing with laughter at the absurdity of the unequal fight. The hopelessness reduced him to hysteria, overcome with levity.

The nurse plunged the needle in his arm and suddenly he saw the noiseless kitten cry face of the one-man band. Mew, mew, and the man held his cupped hand out to Partridge. Not up or down, just out. Horizontal.

# JIMMY THE DANCER: NECROMANCER

*T*he china was so fine that you could see through it, like an old lady's hand against the light of a weak lamp. The pink was as clear as the first hectic flush of a fever and the black patterning and fine black edging to the rim gave it an almost perfect frailty. Pink and black, almost macabre.

The cup and saucer sat on a small silver tray, and by reaching forward across his desk he could flick the edge of the cup with the buckled yellow horn of his fingernail and listen to the china ring. He was a man who was in love with loveliness, beauty, perfection.

It wasn't as if this sensibility prevented him from being an excellent public servant. He was. So good that he was hated. He was incredibly hard when it came to the mechanical dealing with the papers that shifted across his desk. James King was an autocrat, masterfully efficient, totally outside the realm of the lives of the staff below him, held in awe by those above him. James was one apart.

Three things rather separated him from ordinary men – his cup and saucer set on the desk, a nautilus under a bell of glass on the bookshelf and, in the bottom drawer, a violin. Such a hard man, so in love with beauty.

He was large. His face was puffed like an oven-fresh scone. His hair was fair and fine, and he reminded you of one of those huge white gelded cats, a cat that a child would draw with the three letters M O Q. The tail impatiently flicking.

A man whose moments of greatest pleasure were to take a fine china cup in his thickened hands and turn its weird colours this way and that in the light had to shield his treasure. In this game you had to be tough, let no one find you weak.

His wife wore cardigans and worried about the SEC accounts and would challenge the meter reader every second month. What was her beauty? Where had it gone? Waiting patiently for her tirade to end, did the meter reader recognize in this heavy woman with cardigan drawn across her chest, a girl whose tiny breasts had been turned this way and that in the light, by the paws of a huge white cat. A cat that purred against the warmth of her flesh. Did she remember herself? After a while, some things are inconceivable. Inconceivable.

But there was an urgency about the way she did things, and a rose of hectic flushing on the cheek that told of something inconsolable. What is it that robs the chest of fire? There are so many things, so many many ways to let a flame dwindle to the point where it becomes a mere flush of rose, a hint of fever, an ember only chafed into warmth by frustration and SEC accounts.

And his flame was a desultory flicker kept sheltered by such slight things – the frailest china, the paperiness of Nautilus, the trembling tautened strings of a violin.

'Mr King?' There was a woman at his door. Slim, blonde, beautiful; an enemy, a person to make demands, to challenge his authority. He would show her.

She proposed the new project. Completely against the current guidelines, totally within the department's responsibilities.

One fat finger strayed towards the china cup and saucer. He didn't look up from his pudgy hand.

'No.' Flat, nerveless. She laughed and tossed her head back, and he was tricked into looking up. He saw that her hair still swung against the warm flesh of her neck.

She lifted the silver tray away from his outstretched hand and put the sheets of paper before him. Through a blur of rage he saw that it could be done, easily; it had been worked out very well, as well as he could have done, should he want to.

He was going to quote the audit and budget ceilings, but when he looked up again she was smiling at him. Oh, he'd been smiled at before, but a fat man learns to study smiles.

And this woman was smiling right into him. He was bathed in the generous light from her face. Her eyes radiated a warmth like liquor in a crystal glass held before a flame. It was a smile that swept across your heart like the feet of dotterels.

There it was. Beauty. Not just of form and shape but of essence. His trinity of beauties were about him, and here was another. A woman whose eyes sought and found the beads of beauty in his own heart and turned them this way and that in the light of her gaze.

He drew the paper towards him and studied it. He grunted his approval and moved a finger to dismiss her, but as he raised his eyes she was holding his cup in her hand.

'This is very delicate china, Mr King, very beautiful. It avoids being ugly by the finest margin – transcends ugliness.' She left him, and he stood and turned to the window to look out over the darkening city, the gems of light in column office blocks, the black ribbon of river, the derricks and lit-up ships of the port.

He lifted the violin from the drawer and played a concerto to the black lump of trees in the park, to the jewels of the city, the dark hulks of ships at wharves, to the traffic lights and the pigeons whose heads were tucked into the puffed prow of their breasts. He was aware that the door had been left open, and she would be there.

Without turning he asked, 'And is that also beautiful?' He played only moderately well. There was no absolute ascension from the realm of geography. She was no liar.

'It is beautiful that you should play it.'

'Ah,' he said and continued to stare out across the black velvet cut-out of the city. A silhouette against a royal blue sky where stars were like chips of ice.

Time manages to creak its way around watch faces, the illuminations of digital displays flick out new numbers in the night. All those threes, fours, fives gradually build into an hour that becomes an eight, a nine, a ten, which becomes a different day.

And with these accretions of time, the corpses of coral insects are shed from our lives like sloughed skin. People pass. You know how it is. One day you look up and life has changed. You glance at the clock. The threes and fours and fives still flicker there, the hands on the face still point at the same twelve numbers, but it's the revolutions that count. The hands wipe across that face each day – wipe out time, life. You know how it is. You've owned a watch, you've woken in the night, checked the clock and found it to be different. Time has gone away.

And people go away. Moments go away. Beautiful things become mere memories. But if you have a shell, you might preserve it under glass, china can be cradled carefully in soft flesh, even while the flesh itself is dying.

He learnt to adapt some Eric Satie nocturnes for the black city silhouette. He played them and his soul was stoked, but not assuaged. He didn't seem to have within him the beauty that several times he had seen in other things and more rarely in people. He let the bow hang from his hand and his heart ached to play the music of such beauty that trees would weep and the inward spirals of fragile shells blush. To make music that would take the longing from his tongue and draw love to him. To draw love to him, to be sure of love so that he could – place it under glass, set it on a silver tray?

But anyway, the music seemed not to be there.

The chalice in his heart had been invaded by some other thing, something that scrabbled like a crab in a bucket. He could hear the scuttle of its claws in his chest.

He would draw the bow across the strings more urgently, but still his notes had only the steadiness and predictability of the numbers on a digital display. They flicked up correctly. Time was drawn out.

'Good morning, Mr King, I was just passing, and –'

He raised his face to that beautiful smile, and huge drops of old tears slipped across the mounds beneath his eyes, down the curves of his cheeks.

'Mr King –' Her eyes too were flooded with tears. He saw her hand cover the pudgy dough of his fist. 'Mr King – please, James –' James. He looked at the pale and delicate hand placed over his, the bones in the back of the hand like fine porcelain.

'Yes, James – the fiddler – Jimmy the dancer – necro-mancer.' He tapped his chest with one finger like a saveloy bleached white with boiling.

'No –' she said.

'Oh, but I am. Jimmy the Dancer. Dancing to my own tune.' He lifted the cup. 'The necromancer –'

# DREAMING

'*I* thought I dreamt that there was a huge red scar on Australia.'

'You did.'

'That it was like the red stamp of a birth mark, smeared fecundity, a print of designation.'

'It was.'

'I thought I dreamt that all of a sudden it was plain to me what the country was. I passed a shallow lake with desert edges and a land corrugated like the bottom of the sea. And then I came to the mark, a mark not of trade but of destination, an ancient rune. The same as Aborigines will paint and then point to, but provide no explanation. Hold their palms up and just say, "It is there." '

'It is true. It is there.'

'And later I sat up as if in a dream and a mountain thrust itself like the back of a whale out of a snowy plain, and it was like that other rock, the red one I've seen in other dreams. But the white rock had the glow-worm gleams of window lights at its foot, and I stared from another passing window and saw this other wilderness where few men lived. Then, in another passage of the dream, a hand reached out from a city of watery

149

lanes and shook mine. The man's hair was silver, his face benign, and he spoke-shaved wood from ancient chairs. He was a fascist, someone said.'

'Yes he was. Is.'

'This old, upright man, with the son of the careful eyes and hands like worn mahogany blocks, this old man, a fascist, they said. But surely not; he loves the old timbers, he can turn them into useful things, he has known labour and poverty, and *he* wore the black shirt?'

'More so, he joined the fascist police.'

'And yet I liked him. He bought me wine and was concerned that all was well with me. You would call him a good man.'

'Yes, you must.'

'I cannot!'

'But if you say he is a good man, you must call him so.'

'I said he seemed a good man, that if you didn't know you'd call him a good man.'

'Ah.'

'Surely there is a difference.'

'Surely you must call men how they seem after their actions. We have all made actions.'

'Men are so unreliable.'

'Yes, we are.'

'I shall turn my face to the wilderness. Where was that place where the whaleback hill thrust up from snow?'

'Villeneuve, near the Lake of Geneva.'

'Geneva?'

'Yes.'

'And the place where the birth mark is printed on Australia's flank?'

'That is near where the blacks killed Leichhardt, and who knows how many blacks were killed there, just for being there after they'd lost it.'

'The centre –'

'The red heart.'

'And the old man –'

150

'He is a Venetian. The people who fled violence and took up trade and art in an island state.'

'An island?'

'Yes, an island. Like yours. They are all stained.'

'But perhaps some are less injured, have fewer grievances.'

'Fewer grievances perhaps, but no less grief.'

'I will find that red stain.'

'Of course.'

'I shall stand on it.'

'Oh, we always do.'

'I shall know it.'

'Your dominion. It always starts thus.'

'But I shall not disclaim and preclude –'

'Oh yes, I forgot, you are a good man.'

'I am just a man.'

'It is well to remember that.'

'Well, what of you, then?'

'Oh, I saw the stains and the whalebacked mountains, and like you, shall not forget them.'

'And what will you do?'

'Do?'

'About mankind –'

'Oh, mankind? I shall probably do nothing – like you.'

'I told you, I will find both places, and I shall know them, and then I will know what is to be done.'

'And the old man?'

'He is old.'

'Ah, yes, old.'

# ACKNOWLEDGEMENTS

'Sirens' was first published in *A Ream Of Writers*, and broadcast on ABC radio 3LO; 'Cicadas' was first published in the *Canberra Times*; 'Soldier Goes to Ground' in the Sydney *Sun-Herald*; 'Gravity and Levity' in *Mattoid*; 'Funny Man' in *Hat Trick*; 'Thylacine' in *Australian Short Stories* and Sydney *Sun-Herald*. 'Black Velvet Night' won a prize in the Fellowship of Australian Writers' State of Victoria award in 1979, 'Thylacine' in 1984, 'Harold's Trudy' in the McGregor College Literature Competition in 1982, 'Nautilus' in the Begonia Festival of 1981 and 'Sirens' in the 1981 ACTU Henry Lawson Award. The characters in these stories are entirely fictitious, subject as they are to intemperate imagination and the almost invisible accretions of coral insects.

The 'hints' come from those who spent the time to talk, and for their stories and companionship in a desperate world I must thank the Becker family, Arthur Tasker, Col McLeod, Ken Morrison, Koorie cousins from the Murray to Maramingo, Alf Briggs, Lorraine Phelan, Robert Allen, Alan Dunstan and Alf Pascoe.

The language which purports to be of the Kurnai of Gippsland is based more on lyric than fact, but uses the eight or nine real words of that language I have been able to discover. I hear their voices all the time.

Six of these stories were written in the Australia Council's studio in Venice, and all were revised there in preparation for this book – an incomparably bizarre blend of Byzantine stone and Austral rock.